"Are you in love with him?"

Stephanie's eyes flickered, but she didn't answer. "Are you?" Gerard insisted.

"I don't know," she admitted. "I didn't have time to find out. He was the sort of man most girls dream of marrying—"

"Good husband material," he finished for her cynically. "It wasn't love at first sight, then?"

"I don't believe in love at first sight." She felt herself flushing as Gerard eyed her oddly. She had fallen for Gerard at first sight, of course. Stephanie froze, looking up into his hypnotic gray eyes.

"You know you'll be living with me in London." It was a statement that shocked her completely. "I'm not letting you out of my sight until we're married," he said.

It seemed the most insane idea she had heard in her life!

CHARLOTTE LAMB began to write "because it was one job I could do without having to leave the children." Now writing is her profession. She has had more than forty Harlequin novels published since 1978. "I love to write," she explains, "and it comes very easily to me." She and her family live in a beautiful old home on the Isle of Man, between England and Ireland. Charlotte spends eight hours a day working at her typewriter—and she enjoys every minute of it.

Books by Charlotte Lamb

Don't miss any of our special offers. Write to us at the following address for information on our newest releases.

Harlequin Reader Service
901 Fuhrmann Blvd., P.O. Box 1397, Buffalo, NY 14240
Canadian address: P.O. Box 603,
Fort Erie, Ont. L2A 5X3

CHARLOTTE LAMB

love in the dark

Harlequin Books

TORONTO • NEW YORK • LONDON
AMSTERDAM • PARIS • SYDNEY • HAMBURG
STOCKHOLM • ATHENS • TOKYO • MILAN

Harlequin Presents first edition June 1987
ISBN 0-373-10987-3

Original hardcover edition published in 1986
by Mills & Boon Limited

CHAPTER ONE

STEPHANIE STUART handed her key to the woman on the other side of the reception desk, smiling politely. 'I hope you'll be very comfortable here, Mrs Graham. George will bring up your bags immediately. You're on the second floor; take a right turn as you leave the lift, your room is halfway down that corridor.'

'Could I have some tea brought up to my room at once, please?' The grey-haired woman gave a sigh. 'I'm very tired and I'm dying for some tea.'

'Of course, I'll see to that for you at once,' Stephanie nodded, giving the woman a concerned glance. She looked tired; in fact she looked exhausted. 'Is there anything else I can do for you, Mrs Graham? Please don't hesitate to ask, we're here to help our guests.'

'That's very good of you, but all I need is a cup of tea, a warm bath and an hour or two on my bed, then I'll be fine.' Mrs Graham was very thin and pale; her features seemed drawn. Stephanie hoped she wasn't ill. She had seen that look in someone's face before— the bluish lips, the lines of pain. She wouldn't be surprised if Mrs Graham had a heart condition. She watched the woman walk towards the lift, frowning, then wrote on Mrs Graham's private card, PHC. It was the custom of the Wyville Arms to have a careful filing system for all their guests, listing their tastes and preferences, their characters and danger spots. It helped the staff to give a personal service so that if a crotchety retired Army officer arrived he would not be offended by the wrong newspaper in the morning, or by being given China tea when he only drank Indian, or lightly grilled bacon when he liked it crisp.

Stephanie slid Mrs Graham's card into the drawer in which they kept current details. Glancing at her watch, she made a wry face. Anya was late again. It was ten minutes past six; Stephanie should have gone off duty at six, but her replacement, Anya Carter, managed to clip a little time off each end of her shift, arriving late and leaving early unless the manager was around to watch her.

Gill appeared through the door behind Stephanie. 'Coming?' She looked around the lobby. 'Where's Anya?' Catching the expression on Stephanie's face, she groaned. 'Not late again? Really, she is the limit! It's a sauce, she shouldn't be allowed to get away with it.'

'If she isn't here soon I'll have to ring Mr Wood. There's no way I can work late tonight.'

'Of course, you're going to a party, aren't you?'

'Elspeth's engagement party! I'm not missing that. Mrs Cameron would never forgive me.' Stephanie spoke lightly, but she was half serious. Mrs Cameron could be very kind and pleasant, but she had a rigid, unbending sense of what she expected from people and Stephanie was slightly scared of her. She had accepted an invitation to Elspeth's party; Mrs Cameron would expect her to be there.

'Mrs Cameron? Don't you mean Euan?' teased Gill.

Laughing, Stephanie shook her head.

'Oh, I see—you can handle him, but not his mother?'

'Something like that.' Stephanie's blue eyes danced; her wide mouth curving with a happiness which made

Gill smile back at her.

'You're serious about him, aren't you? Think it's *the* one? The real thing?' She sounded half envious; Gill Evans had just broken up with her boy-friend and was going through a trough of depression and self-doubt which made her slightly moody.

Stephanie crossed her fingers behind her back. 'Maybe—who knows? I'm not rushing it.' Her eyes flashed behind Gill and she gave a little sigh of relief, seeing Anya slipping into the reception area. 'Oh, there you are! You're nearly fifteen minutes late—it really isn't on, Anya. I've got an important date tonight.'

Anya had her excuse ready, glib and coaxing. 'Oh, I'm sorry, Stevie, but the bus was running late, it wasn't my fault, honestly.'

Stephanie and Gill exchanged looks. 'You'd better take an earlier bus in future, Anya. That one seems to run late at least once a week.' The mild sarcasm was water off a duck's back, Anya merely smiled, and Stephanie had no more time to waste on her tonight.

She rushed into the staff-room to grab her coat and then she and Gill made their way to the hotel entrance. A taxi drew up and disgorged a new guest. Idly, Stephanie watched him get out, turning his head to glance at the meter in the taxi, the wind whipping his blond hair backwards, revealing a sculptured profile, coolly incisive.

A spasm of shock made her stomach muscles clench. It couldn't be! Fate couldn't do this to her.

Gill was staring too, unashamedly, her lips pursed in a low whistle. 'Isn't he something?' she whispered as her feet slowed so that she could take a longer look. 'I hope he's staying here—were we expecting another guest tonight? You don't know his name, do you?'

Stephanie didn't answer. She was already some feet away, moving so fast she was almost running. She didn't look back, but she didn't have to—she knew his name, and the hotel certainly hadn't been expecting him. She wouldn't have missed that name on the list of expected guests, it would have leapt out at her like a snake from a box.

Gill caught up with her at the car, panting breathlessly. 'You *are* in a hurry to get away!'

You can say that again, Stephanie thought, unlocking the car. What on earth was he doing here? He hadn't booked, it must be a one-night casual, perhaps he was *en route* somewhere, and would move on in the morning. Thank God he hadn't arrived ten minutes earlier when she was on the desk. She slid into the driving seat, angrily aware that she was trembling. The very prospect of looking up, innocently unaware, to find herself staring at him across the reception desk made her blood turn to ice.

'I hope he isn't just a one-nighter,' said Gill, clipping her safety belt. 'He didn't look like a travelling salesman, did he? Let's hope he's still here on Monday.'

Let's hope he isn't, Stephanie thought, starting the engine. As she drove out of the car park she saw the taxi doing a U-turn in the road to drive away. Their new guest had vanished, but they both saw the porter, George, his hands gripping the handles of two very expensive pigskin suitcases, shouldering his way through the swing doors.

'Like the luggage,' Gill commented, peering. 'That's real pigskin, isn't it? He must be loaded. I bet he's married, but then the best men always are.'

She seemed unaware of Stephanie's silence and chattered lightly as they drove through Wyville's Saturday night traffic. The hotel was just off the sea front, but from some of the bedrooms on the upper floors you could get stunning sea views. The little town was not a popular resort now, although it had been at the turn of the century during the heyday of Victorian seaside holidays, a fact reflected in much of the architecture, including that of the Wyville Arms. Solidly built, but with many curlicues; turrets at the corners, high windows, gables on the top floor, a mass of ornamental plasterwork, the hotel was far too large for the custom it got now. They relied heavily on passing traffic; often half the rooms were empty.

Wyville was something of a backwater. Streets of crumbling Edwardian boarding-houses spread out from the sea front; few of them did much business, even in the high season. Now, in early spring, many of them were closed until the start of the summer, their windows blank, their paintwork shabby. The little town had a melancholy air, like a bride deserted at the altar, her finery decaying, her guests long gone, her future bleak.

Stephanie shivered, and Gill stopped talking to give her a sideways frown. 'Hey, are you okay? You look pale, I hadn't noticed.'

'Tired, I suppose,' Stephanie said with a forced smile as she turned into the new housing estate on the edge of town. Gill lived with her parents in one of the timber and concrete boxes set in pocket-handkerchief gardens. Pulling up outside, Stephanie turned towards her passenger.

'Have a good weekend.'

'Same to you. Don't drink too much at the party or

Mrs Cameron will decide you aren't a suitable daughter-in-law!'

Stephanie managed to laugh, although that wasn't really funny. 'I've only been dating Euan for three months—hold on there! Marriage hasn't even been discussed.'

Gill winked. 'Thought about, though, I bet.' She got out, slamming the door with an enthusiasm that made Stephanie wince. Her head had begun to throb; she hoped she wasn't getting the sort of headache that hangs around all evening. That would ruin the party.

It was ruined already, she admitted grimly, driving away. She had been looking forward to tonight all week and now she wished she wasn't going out. She needed to be alone for a few hours to think; her mind was being eaten alive with questions. What was he doing here? Did he know she lived and worked in Wyville? How long was he staying and was it sheer chance that had brought him here or . . .

She broke off, taking a deep anxious breath, her face white. It had to be mere coincidence; it mustn't be anything else. She wouldn't even consider the other alternative. Yet she had a sinking sense of uneasiness about seeing him outside the hotel where she worked. Her life was just beginning to hold a new happiness; the old nightmares had faded into memory. Surely fate could not be so cruel as to bring them all back?

She was so obsessed with anxiety that she almost missed the turning which led to her home. Realising it, she braked suddenly, skidding on the wet tarmac. It had been raining that afternoon, obviously. She hadn't noticed, she had been too busy.

As she took the right-hand turn a car behind her hooted noisily. She looked into her driving mirror,

face apologetic, and then saw that it was Robert
following her in his new Ford. She waved and drove
on to park outside the house. Robert turned his car
into the short driveway and pulled up, leaning out of
the window.

'Trying to kill someone? What were you dreaming
about when you should have been keeping your mind
on the road? Or should I say who?' He grinned, brown
eyes teasing, as Stephanie slid out of her driving seat
and came walking towards him.

Strangers might never have guessed that they were
brother and sister. They resembled each other only in
having the same colour hair—a warm, rich dark
brown close to the colour of polished mahogany.
Robert was solidly built, a man of thirty with a rugged
face, individual if not handsome features, and a casual
good humour. Stephanie was slight, her body slender
and supple, innately graceful. Her features had a
delicacy which was faintly deceptive; she was not
quite as vulnerable as she seemed, but her blue eyes
had an occasional sadness, as if something haunted
her, and her long, pale throat made her seem fragile.

'You're early,' she said as Robert joined her.
'Hospital kick you out for killing patients?'

'By some fluke they all survived today,' he replied,
sauntering beside her towards the front door. 'I did my
best, but we had a tough bunch in the theatre, they
kept insisting on staying alive.'

'Gwen's on the night shift, isn't she?'

He nodded. His wife worked in the same hospital
but all too often on a different shift, so that she and
Robert practically had to make an appointment to
meet for lunch once a week. Gwen always said that
they had been able to see more of each other before

they got married than they did now.

'The powers that be have this thing about married couples getting together, you know. Sex scares the hell out of them. They're determined to keep us apart so we can't do anything they don't approve of!'

She laughed. 'Poor Robert, I can see the frustration is murder.'

He made a face at her. 'Okay, laugh. Wait until you've married a doctor. You won't think its so funny then, always being on different shifts.' He unlocked the front door and Stephanie walked into the hall. She had a separate flat on the upper floor, above the garage, but while Gwen was on the night shift Stephanie usually got Robert his evening meal. He always protested that he could manage to put something frozen into the microwave all on his own, but Stephanie preferred to cook a real meal for them, something a good deal more nutritious than an instant TV dinner.

'I wish everyone would stop marrying Euan and me off,' she said irritably, and her brother looked at her with enquiry in his eyes.

'What's up, doc?'

She laughed. 'Oh, nothing.' She couldn't tell him whom she had seen that evening at the hotel; Robert had enough problems on his mind, he didn't need hers too. She owed Robert so much; more than she could ever repay. He had stood by her when she had needed someone to believe in her, someone to lean on—well, that had been five years ago, she had been very young then. Now she felt very old. She was certainly old enough to shoulder her own worries without landing her brother with their burden. He had a wife to take care of now.

'You haven't quarrelled with Euan, have you?' probed Robert. Stephanie looked amazed and then laughed.

'Of course not!'

'No, I can't imagine Euan quarrelling with anyone, he's Mr Cool in person, isn't he? It's that mother of his, of course—she's so well bred she makes me nervous. I'm sure Euan was a perfect child; he wouldn't have dared be anything else.'

Stephanie gave him an anxious look. 'Don't you like Mrs Cameron?'

'What's there to dislike? Always courteous, always reasonable—my God, I wouldn't have the nerve to dislike her, it would be positively ill-mannered.' Robert walked towards the stairs. 'I'm going to have a long soak in the bath, a glass of whisky and half an hour's absolute total idleness. After that I may feel like going to Elspeth's party, which at the moment I am not eager to do. Out of the last twenty-four hours I've worked seventeen. I suppose I ought to be grateful for the fact that I'm not a surgeon and don't have to stand on my feet all day. At least the anaesthetist gets to sit down. Let us give thanks for small mercies.'

His voice trailed up the stairs after his disappearing figure and Stephanie looked after him with affection and concern. Robert had been working these hours for months; how much more could he take? His salary was derisory, he needed the rent Stephanie paid for her three rooms, in order to help pay the mortgage on this house, and all the money Gwen earned as a staff nurse went into a special fund intended to make it possible for her to give up work in two years' time in order to have a baby. They had planned their life like a military operation, down to the last detail—but

Stephanie couldn't help wondering if either of them had realised how exhausting and frustrating these years were going to be.

She went into the kitchen and prepared the salad which she was going to serve with a quick cheese soufflé. While the soufflé was cooking, she ran into her own flat to get ready for the party. A quick shower, into her coral-pink silk dress, and ten minutes in front of her dressing-table mirror, then she was ready to rush back to the kitchen. She heard the water running out of Robert's bath and called to him.

'Dinner will be on the table in ten minutes exactly.'

'Right.'

'Don't forget, you're to wear your evening suit. No excuses. We may go on somewhere afterwards, dancing, late supper—who knows?'

'Gwen said that if she gets off promptly at ten she might catch up with us if we go to the Laserlight.'

'In her uniform?' She peered up the stairs at him and Robert craned over the banisters to grimace at her.

'No, dummy. She'll change at the hospital. She took her new dress with her.'

'Get dressed!' she hissed, seeing that he was still in his damp towelling robe.

'Nag, nag, nag!' Robert vanished and Stephanie went back into the kitchen to gaze anxiously at the clock. If he didn't hurry, her soufflé would be ruined. It had to be eaten the minute it came out of the oven or all that soaring lightness would collapse into a puddle.

She checked the table by the window for the second time; she hadn't forgotten anything. Where was Robert? Then she heard his running feet on the stairs and with a sigh of relief grabbed up her oven gloves.

An hour and a half later they drove up the hill towards Cameron House, a Victorian extravaganza of turrets and Gothic battlements, built at the same time as the similar houses in Wyville, by a speculative builder from Edinburgh called Hamish Cameron. He had decided to settle here and built himself a large house on a hill overlooking Wyville so that he could contemplate his own achievements from a great height. Hamish Cameron had lived to be ninety-five, married for the third time at the age of sixty, and finally managed to get himself a son and heir, Hamish the Second, who was so dominated by the old man that he grew up a nervous wreck. Hamish the Second had dreamt of becoming an artist. His father had brought a stick down on his head and ordered him to join the firm. He had also ordered him to marry his cousin, Margo. Hamish obeyed, but he died young, collapsing of a heart attack when he was forty-three while swimming in the sea with his own small son, Euan. 'My father had a sad life,' Euan had once told Stephanie. 'Even after his old tyrant of a father died, Dad couldn't give up business and start painting because there was no one to run the firm.'

When her husband died, however, Margo Cameron took over control of the building firm and ran it with immense success, intending to hand it over to her own son when he grew up. Euan had other ideas. He had wanted to be a doctor from the day he saw his father dying on the beach at Wyville. Euan was a quiet, gentle and affectionate boy. His mother didn't imagine she would have any difficulties with him, but Euan had inherited an iron will from her. She couldn't persuade him out of his intention to go to medical school. Euan qualified and got a job in the hospital at

Wyville, working in the cardiology department, specialising in heart operations because his father's death had made that an obsession with him. His mother went on successfully running the family firm.

The party tonight was to celebrate the engagement of Euan's sister, Elspeth, to John Barry, an architect who had worked on the new housing estate with Mrs Cameron. Their marriage would give Johnny a golden future with the firm, but it would also give Mrs Cameron what Euan had denied her—a member of the family to help her run the firm in future. Cynics in the town had murmured that it was an arranged marriage, more business than romance. They didn't know Elspeth. Stephanie did; and knew that Elspeth was deeply in love with Johnny. His feelings were not so obvious; he didn't wear his heart on his sleeve.

As Robert parked in the only space left available on the long driveway up to the house, he looked at the lighted windows and above them the bizarre silhouette of the roof against the moonlit sky. 'Looks like a set for a Hammer horror film, doesn't it? Any minute we'll probably see the bats swooping up from the chimneys.'

'It isn't exactly an ideal home,' Stephanie agreed, sliding her long shapely legs out of the car and standing up.

'You and Euan wouldn't be expected to live here, would you?' enquired Robert, locking the car, and she looked irritably at him across the top of the car.

'Robert! For heaven's sake, stop trying to marry us off. And don't drop any of your loaded hints to Mrs Cameron. Or Euan, come to that. I'll kill you if you do!'

She had enough on her mind tonight without the

added problem of her brother making embarrassing jokes about wedding bells for her and Euan. She no longer felt like going to this party: how could she relax and enjoy herself when she didn't know why Gerard Tenniel was in town and how long he would be staying? She had thought she had put all that behind her, but here he was, a lethal time bomb ticking away, which might at any moment explode and blow her carefully built new life to smithereens.

'I'm sorry, kid, don't get so upset—of course I won't say a word. What do you take me for?'

'Don't tempt me,' she said as they walked towards the house, but she linked her arm through Robert's to show that she forgave him.

He pressed her arm against his side, looking down sideways at her, smiling. 'I just want you to be happy, Stevie. You had a tough time a few years back, I know how badly you felt, but all that is over now and forgotten and I'm glad you're dating Euan, he's a good man. I don't mean to jump ahead of you, or rush you, believe me. I'll try to be discreet tonight.' He put a finger on his mouth. 'My lips are sealed, okay?'

'Okay,' she said, nudging him with her shoulder. 'You are an idiot, you know, but as a brother you're a bargain.'

He laughed. 'I'm not sure how to take that.'

The front door opened; Euan appeared, framed in light, his red hair glinting vividly above the formal evening dress he wore. Mrs Cameron was old-fashioned in many ways—for special occasions like tonight she believed in formal dress, and none of her family would dream of disobeying her.

'Hallo, you look lovely,' said Euan, kissing her lightly as she moved from her brother to greet him.

'My mother's favourite colour, pink; she has a whole bed full of roses just that shade, she'll love that dress.'

'They called it coral, in the dress shop,' Stephanie said, glancing down at the clinging silk. She had chosen a demure style, one she felt Mrs Cameron would approve of—the neckline was modestly scooped a little, the sleeves were puffed, the skirt covered her knees. She was uneasily aware, though, that the material adhered a little too closely to her figure. She might be covered up but somehow the thin silk gave a very different impression. When she tried it on in the shop she hadn't noticed how seductively silk clung, how sensuous an impression it gave, or she would never have chosen this dress. But perhaps Mrs Cameron would be too busy with her guests to notice.

'Hallo, Rob. Pretty rigorous day we had, wasn't it?' Euan said, grinning past her at her brother. 'Do you feel as whacked as I do?'

'Worse,' said Robert. 'I got that long lecture from Sister Morris about going to sleep while they were wheeling in the next patient. I closed my eyes for a second and Morris hit me like a whirlwind. That woman is beyond a joke! She's never forgiven me for marrying Gwen. She hates her theatre nurses to get married—all they're supposed to have on their minds is work.'

'Is Gwen going to manage to get here tonight?'

'Doubt it. She hopes to get off at ten, but she may not manage it if there's an emergency and when she does she'll be on call until two. Never marry a nurse!'

Stephanie tensed, hoping that her brother wasn't going to deliver one of his jokey hints, but Robert's smile was free of any double meaning and Euan laughed.

'Working in theatre all I ever see is their eyes, and I don't get turned on by a pair of eyes above a mask.' He looked at Stephanie thoughtfully, as if just noticing her eyes. 'You never wanted to be a nurse, Stevie?'

She shook her head. 'Blood makes me faint.'

Both men grinned. 'Most people do pass out, their first time in theatre,' said Euan, putting an arm around her to steer her into the house. He looked down at the parcel she was carrying. 'That for Elspeth and Johnny?'

She nodded. She had taken most of her lunch hour to find what she was looking for—a boxed set of Waterford sherry glasses. She wanted a particular design which had not been stocked by the first two shops she visited, but eventually she had tracked these down in a smaller shop on the edge of town.

Euan looked good in evening dress; it did something for his thin, wiry figure. Although he worked hard, hours as long as Robert's, he still found time to keep fit with punishing games of squash and tennis at the hospital staff sports centre, built with Cameron money five years ago, at Euan's suggestion. Stephanie had picked up a strong suggestion of disapproval from Mrs Cameron, who disliked spending money too freely, but in that, as in choosing his career, Euan had had his way. His quiet determination was visible in his bony, controlled face; patients could read nothing in his calm smile and steady hazel eyes. Euan wasn't handsome by any means, but his strength attracted Stephanie. He was a man you could rely on; someone you trusted implicitly. That, in her view, was more important than good looks.

The party had spread throughout the ground floor of the house. Stephanie knew some of the other guests

but others were complete strangers, many of them
Cameron relatives whom, Euan said drily, even he
barely knew. His mother had organised this party and
drawn up the guest list. Her future son-in-law was on
display to her family and friends. Johnny's family was
here, and several of his friends, but by and large, the
Cameron contingent dominated the gathering.

'Hallo, Stephanie, nice of you to come.' Elspeth
floated over to kiss her, floated being the exact word to
describe the way she moved on very high, silvery
sandals, her pale green and white chiffon dress
drifting around her in a delicious swirl. She was only
five feet tall, even with those high heels; her hair, a
shade lighter than her brother's, had a red-gold
brilliance, and her eyes were mint green. She was
much younger than Euan and her features had a soft,
rounded curve to them, but behind the youth and
smiling sweetness lay the same Cameron determination. Elspeth was no soft touch, as Johnny would
discover after their marriage.

'I hope you and Johnny are going to be blissfully
happy,' said Stephanie, handing over her foil-
wrapped gift.

'Oh, a prezzie!' Elspeth cooed, pulling at the gold
ribbon bow. 'You are an angel, thank you, they're
gorgeous, just what we wanted—how did you
remember?'

Elspeth had spent the last few weeks making lists of
all the things she would need to set up home in the
personally designed house which was now being built
by the firm for her and Johnny. Stephanie hadn't had
to use any imagination; Elspeth knew precisely what
she wanted, and made sure everyone else did too. She
was very like her mother.

Robert had a gift with him, too. While he was giving it to Elspeth, Euan guided Stephanie over to say hallo to his mother, who was holding court from her Queen Anne chair at the other side of the room.

'Good evening, Stephanie.' Mrs Cameron raised her face so that Stephanie could kiss her cheek. She always carried a faint, delicate fragrance of lavender around with her, seeming never to wear any other perfume. The perfume matched her conservative clothes: tonight she wore a cool blue evening dress with long sleeves and a high neckline which hid her finely lined throat. The style and material could have been worn at any time in the last twenty years, Stephanie thought wryly. She wouldn't be surprised to hear that Mrs Cameron had had the dress as long as that, either.

'You look very daring tonight,' Mrs Cameron said with slight reproof, eyeing the clinging silk dress.

'Oh, Mother, really!' protested Euan, laughing. 'Stevie looks marvellous and that's a very pretty colour—you've always said how much you like pink.'

'Yes,' his mother said uncertainly. Her eyes were almost the same colour as her son's and her hair had been auburn. Now it was a becoming silver, softly curled around her very feminine features. She had a small, delicate nose, high cheekbones and a bow of a mouth lightly glossed with pale pink. She must have been very pretty as a girl, Stephanie thought, but all that femininity was deceptive. Under her sweet smile, Mrs Cameron had a backbone of steel. All the same, she was never unkind or spiteful. She had high standards and insisted on maintaining them, insisted everyone around her should maintain them, too. She wasn't easy to live up to, nor, probably, to live with—

but Stephanie respected her, and rather liked her too.

'Find Stephanie a glass of sherry, Euan, but don't monopolise her. No skulking in corners together tonight; this is a family party. Everyone will want to meet her. Your Aunt Jennifer was asking me about her earlier. Where is she?' Mrs Cameron glanced around the crowded room, her eye moving quickly over the little groups of chattering people, until they rested on a couple sitting on a sofa talking. 'Oh, there she is—with Adrian. Doesn't he look well? You would never believe that he was over seventy. He swims before breakfast every day, he tells me. You might try that, Euan, in that expensive sports centre you persuaded me to build. You might as well use it occasionally.'

'I use it every day, Mother. We all do. It's probably done more good than anything else we've added to the hospital facilities in the last fifty years. Preventative medicine is worth . . .'

'Euan, please! No lectures, not tonight. I know your views on preventative medicine. Take Stephanie over to meet Jennifer and your cousin Adrian.'

Euan gave a wry smile. 'I'll get you that drink first, Stevie. You're going to need it. Aunt Jennifer can only be taken in small doses with the help of a stiff drink.'

His mother looked reprovingly at him. 'Really, Euan! That wasn't very kind. And it seems a great pity to shorten Stephanie's pretty name in that way. You make her sound like a boy!'

'In that dress, nobody is going to mistake her for a boy,' a deep, cool voice murmured behind them.

Stephanie swung round, all the colour rushing out of her face, and the tall man who had spoken observed her with a lazy mockery that had the quality of dry ice.

His smile was spiked with menace and Stephanie swallowed in sheer panic. Oh, God, what was he doing here?

'Gerard! How wonderful to see you again. I'm so glad you could come.' Mrs Cameron's voice was warm; she held out her hand, smiling.

'Hallo, Godmother.' He bent his blond head to kiss her hand lightly. 'You look charming, and you haven't changed a hair since I last saw you. How do you do it? Have you discovered the secret of eternal youth?'

Mrs Cameron laughed as he straightened. 'Nonsense, Gerard. Such flattery! I'm past the age for such delightful compliments.'

'I don't believe it.'

Stephanie was fighting for self-control, her hands tensely clasped together. He was Mrs Cameron's godson? His name had never been mentioned by anyone here before. She had no idea. So that was why he had checked into the hotel—he had been invited to this party. Had he known that he would find her here? He hadn't seemed surprised; indeed, his smile had had a twist of satisfaction as he observed her stunned dismay, as though he had been looking forward to that moment when she first set eyes on him. He'd known just how much of a shock that would be, and he had enjoyed watching her face.

Well, he had had his fun. She wished she had been able to hide how she felt, but he had taken her by surprise. She might be five years older than the last time they met; but her control over her emotions was no stronger.

'You remember my son, Euan, don't you?' Mrs Cameron was murmuring. 'Euan, this is Gerard Tenniel—his mother was my best friend at school and he's my godson. You met him several times when you were younger, do you remember?'

'Of course,' said Euan, offering his hand without visible enthusiasm.

He had never heard that name on Stephanie's lips, he couldn't know that she had ever met this man before, but as the two men shook hands they eyed each other with remote courtesy, as though Euan had picked up some vibration in the air. Or perhaps he had never liked Gerard Tenniel much, anyway? She must not read too much into Gerard's presence here. He might not have any intention of revealing her past. He knew Mrs Cameron; he knew just what effect that old story would have—he couldn't be cruel enough to wreck her chance of happiness with Euan.

The blond head turned her way, the cool, grey eyes travelled up and down her body in a speculation which was little short of insolence. 'Aren't you going to introduce us, Godmother?' he drawled, and Stephanie hardly dared to breathe as Mrs Cameron answered.

'Of course, how remiss of me—Gerard, this is Stephanie Stuart, I'm sure I mentioned her when I wrote to your mother with the invitation, she's been seeing a good deal of Euan lately.'

Gerard Tenniel held out his hand. He was pretending that they were strangers. He wasn't going to tell them what he knew about her. She was afraid to hope too much, but her blue eyes reflected fear and pleading as she let her hand be engulfed by his, and he smiled with a mocking satisfaction that made it clear that Gerard Tenniel had a whip poised over her head. He might not plan to tell them yet—but that was no guarantee that she was safe. She could not trust this man.

CHAPTER TWO

STEPHANIE hardly knew how she got through the next hour. It felt as if she had sleepwalked her way round the room. People spoke to her, she smiled at them without really seeing them, nodding. Did she answer? She must have done, yet she couldn't remember anything she said. Her heart was beating with a wild, erratic beat. If she had dared, she would have fled, got away from there, from that house, from Gerard Tenniel. But how could she leave the party? Euan would be puzzled, he might start asking questions and the longer she put off having to answer him the better. If Gerard Tenniel did tell the family what he knew, that would be the end for her and Euan. Stephanie was certain of that.

At least during the time while she and Euan were circulating among his family, she could keep away from Gerard. She didn't look towards him, yet she always knew where he was; from time to time, she picked up the timbre of his deep voice. Five years ago, the sound of that voice made her knees give. Today, it made her feel sick with dread.

'You okay, Stevie? You look a bit green,' said Robert in her ear, and she jumped about ten feet into the air.

'Oh . . .'

'Hey, your nerves are bad! What's up?'

'Nothing, don't be silly,' she said, trying to laugh, but she couldn't fool her brother.

'Quarrelled with Euan?' he asked shrewdly.

'Of course not. I'm just tired.'

'You need to sit down.' Her brother glanced around the room, making a face. 'No empty seats here.' The Cameron relatives were mainly older people who preferred to sit down even at a party. Every chair was taken.

'It doesn't matter, I'm not going to faint.'

'From the look on your face you might, at any minute.' Robert pushed her through the door and across the hall to sit on the stairs.

Stephanie's body collapsed with relief and she gave Robert a wry look.

'Thank you, Doctor.'

'My pleasure. Feel better? It's cooler out here—fewer pairs of lungs using up all the oxygen. That might account for it, you know. People often faint at parties or big gatherings, solely due to lack of air.' He put his hand on the back of her neck. 'Put your head down on your knees, that will bring the blood back to your head in no time.'

She obeyed ruefully. There was no point in telling Robert that it wasn't lack of oxygen making her pale but was a surfeit of Gerard Tenniel. He wouldn't have recognised the name, but Robert knew all about the man and she did not want him to realise who was here tonight. If she could only keep very still and quiet she might be safe. Gerard would go away again and nobody here need ever know about the past. Or was that just wishful thinking? Could anything be buried for ever?

Robert said softly, 'Stay here. I'll get you a glass of water.'

Stephanie closed her eyes, her forehead resting on

her knees. The sound of the party seemed far away. It was sheer bliss to be alone; not to have to smile, talk, pretend. She couldn't stay here long, though—Euan would start wondering where she had got to, and then he would come looking for her.

She heard the door open and the noise of the party grow louder. That must be Euan, coming in search of her. The door shut again as she slowly lifted her head, but it wasn't Euan coming across the dim hall, it was Gerard Tenniel.

She sat up, shaking helplessly, but screwing up her courage to face him. She must not let him see how much he frightened her.

'I wondered where you'd got to,' he muttered, his mouth twisting. 'I thought you might have left altogether.'

'I was hot,' she said, trying not to let her voice tremble. 'I came out here to cool down.'

His grey eyes assessed her, a spark of savagery in their black pupils. 'You look cool enough to me . . . but then you always were deceptive.' He smiled, but the movement of his cold, beautiful mouth made her wince. 'Not to say a bloody little liar,' he added conversationally.

The pretence that they were strangers had vanished; enmity showed in his face and Stephanie looked away, downwards, her lashes fluttering against her cold skin. She couldn't hold that stare; it tortured her.

'Look at me when I'm talking to you!' His hand shot out and caught her chin and she gave a cry of shock at the touch of his fingers. He ruthlessly pushed her head backwards until she was looking up into his icy grey eyes.

'Please . . . my brother will be back any minute,' she whispered, and he stared at her, frowning.

'We've got to talk—if not here, where?'

Stephanie's mind was a blank. She helplessly shook her head and at that second heard Robert's footsteps coming from the kitchen. Gerard heard them, too. He let go of her chin and straightened, pushing his hands into his pockets and taking on a casual air, as though they were having a polite chat: a little small talk between strangers met at a party.

'Come to the hotel,' he hissed so that only she would hear.

Stephanie's pallor increased. 'When?'

'Tomorrow morning, early. We'll have breakfast together.'

His smile made her bite her lower lip. 'I can't . . .'

The smile vanished; his mouth was hard and hostile. 'You'd better be there. Eight o'clock tomorrow morning.'

Before she could answer that, Robert came into sight. He looked surprised when he saw Gerard, but smiled cheerfully. 'Hallo. Did you leave the party for some air, too? It is stuffy in there.' He handed his sister the glass of water; he had dropped a few ice cubes in for good measure, they clinked against the glass as he put it into her hand. 'Here you are, Stevie; feeling any better?'

'Yes, thanks,' she managed huskily, but her brother's professional eye was moving over her and he was frowning.

'You certainly don't look it. I think perhaps I ought to take you home. You may be incubating something.'

The door behind them opened again and Euan came out; his eyes fixing on them in surprise. 'Oh, there you are, Stevie—what's wrong? Aren't you well?'

'She looks to me as if she's coming down with something,' Robert told him.

'I'm fine,' Stephanie insisted, standing up. Gerard took the glass from her and she gave him a quick, nervous glance, but his face was impassive now. He looked calmly sympathetic, indeed. He had accused her of being deceptive—he was more than that, he was a born actor. Nobody would guess that there was anything between them but a brief acquaintance.

'Maybe we shouldn't go on to the club,' said Euan to Robert.

They moved together, stepping slightly apart to have a professional debate, and Stephanie suddenly felt like laughing hysterically. Her emotions were completely out of key.

'The lasers might give her a headache,' agreed Robert, nodding.

'If she hasn't got one already,' Euan said, glancing at her. He came back, put a hand on her forehead. 'Any headache, Stevie?'

'No, I'm fine, of course I'll come on to the club—I don't want to ruin the party.' She had been looking forward to it all week; it wasn't often that they all went out in a group. It wasn't often that Euan had any time off for dancing. Their dates were often a snatched couple of hours at some ridiculous time of the day or evening: a meal somewhere or a cuddle in front of the television in her flat, or merely a walk along the sea front until Euan had to hurry back to the operating theatre to plunge back into work again.

'It seems a little unwise,' Gerard Tenniel murmured coolly.

The two doctors looked at him, professional hackles up. Euan said smilingly, 'I think my mother was asking where you'd got to, Gerard.' His tone said politely that Gerard and his opinions were unwanted.

His mouth crooked with sardonic amusement, Gerard strolled away. Robert stared after him.

'What does he do for a living?'

'Law,' said Euan tersely.

'Solicitor?'

'Barrister.'

Robert shrugged, dismissing Gerard Tenniel. The two men exchanged looks. Who did he think he was? A barrister giving his opinion on a purely medical matter? Typical! Outsiders were always dispensing crazy advice when they knew nothing about the subject. Stephanie knew their views inside out, she had heard them talking impatiently about the nutty ideas people got into their heads about medicine. No other profession was so beset by amateurs interfering in matters best left to the professionals, the trained men and women who knew what they were talking about. At least, that was how Euan and Robert saw it.

They looked back at her, eyes assessing, and she gave them a rueful smile. Now that Gerard was no longer around she felt a little better; her colour was not so deadly and her body was more at ease.

'She's looking better,' they agreed.

'A walk in the fresh air wouldn't do any harm,' Euan said, taking her hand. 'Come on, I prescribe a little exercise.' His eyes teased. 'Accompanied by your private physician!'

Stephanie laughed, letting him draw her towards the front door. 'Your mother will wonder where we are.'

'I'll cover for you,' promised Robert, grinning. 'I'll tell her Stephanie almost fainted and you're dealing with it.'

The night was crisp and cool; the moon laid a silvery wash over trees and houses, giving a magical air to everyday, familiar things. Everything was very still; not a branch moved, not a grass stirred. You could almost hear the sea—a distant murmur as if someone breathed softly across the flat fields.

Euan put his arm around her waist and she leaned on him, her head brushing his shoulder, as they walked, slowly, over the gravel paths and lawns.

He halted to look back at the house, his expression wryly affectionate. 'Crazy old house. I love it, you know. It's a monstrosity, but at least it isn't one of those ticky-tacky boxes we're always building today. They aren't meant to last, you know. They're built to fall down in a few years; cheap materials, run up as fast as possible. There's no pride in workmanship any more, no desire to make a house special or beautiful. That's one reason why I wouldn't go into the firm. Even if I hadn't been set on becoming a heart specialist I would have wanted to find another job. I didn't want anything to do with the sort of houses we were putting up all around Wyville.'

Stephanie watched his thin profile achingly. Euan was a good man, a little stern, at times, high-principled and serious about the things he felt mattered, but a man she respected and admired. He had turned his back on material success to become a doctor because of those high principles. How could she harbour a secret wish that Euan was not quite so serious-minded?

He looked down at her, smiling. 'You look very

sober. Still feeling faint?'

'No, I was thinking ... when Elspeth has got married, there'll only be you and your mother in the house. Won't you feel like two peas rattling around a giant box?'

His eyes held warmth and amusement. 'My grandfather built this place to hold a big family,' he agreed. 'Stevie ...' His hand caressed her cheek and she suddenly knew that he was about to propose.

She couldn't let him, not now. She walked on, talking lightly over her shoulder.

'Elspeth's new house isn't ticky-tacky, though, is it? She's obviously going to have a beautiful home. Johnny's a very good architect; I love the way he's designed the layout of the house.'

She had been waiting for Euan to propose for weeks. Everyone around them seemed to regard it as a settled thing, they were the butt of teasing jokes among their friends and it was true that they had something special—a warmth and sympathy which was even more important than the strong physical attraction they had felt from the beginning. Euan wasn't the type to rush into anything, though. He had taken his time to think it out, and Stephanie had approved of that. Marriage was a serious matter; she didn't want to rush into it either. At the same time, she had expected Euan to say something soon, and now she must not let him.

Gerard Tenniel's arrival on the scene had changed everything, wrecked the settled happiness of her life over the past year or so. It had taken her years to get over what had happened, but now that she had, Gerard had crashed into her life again, bringing back all the bad memories.

When Euan heard about what happened five years ago, how would he look at her? Gerard would paint a very black picture. Even if Euan listened to her side of the story, how could he ever feel the same about her again? What he had just said about his house applied equally to his pride in his family name. The Camerons were still the most important people in this little town, not only because of their wealth, but because of their enormous impact in community life over the past century. Cameron money had built the hospital, equipped new wards, helped to finance the construction of a new church. Mrs Cameron was a justice of the peace, as well as employing a large workforce from the town. Euan's work at the hospital was a source of great pride locally: they saw him as their own doctor, born and bred here but with a reputation as a surgeon which was becoming far more widespread. Euan was a brilliant heart surgeon.

Scandal had never touched their name. How could she bear to be the first to bring scandal to the Cameron family? She should have realised from the beginning that this might happen one day. She had thought that by burying herself here in this little backwater she could bury the past, too, but sooner or later every stone is turned, every secret uncovered.

If she had told Euan the truth at the beginning they might have had a chance; if he believed her side of the story. But she hadn't dared risk it. She had been afraid that he wouldn't want to see her again, even if he had believed her. It wasn't just Euan she had to convince, of course. There was his mother. Mrs Cameron would be deeply shocked, horrified, even if she heard the slightest hint of scandal attached to Stephanie's name. Anyone who joined the Cameron family had to be above suspicion, like Caesar's wife.

Euan caught up with her just before they reached the door. He framed her flushed face with his hands and smiled at her, kissing her nose. 'Shy, darling? Don't be. I won't insist on an answer yet. Think about it. I reckon we make a great team.'

She managed a smile; it wasn't easy, but it seemed to convince Euan.

'That's better,' he murmured, kissing her lips, and then they went back into the house, walking straight into Gerard Tenniel who was in the hall, shrugging into his smooth, black cashmere overcoat.

'Going already?' asked Euan, surprised.

The grey eyes held an ironic gleam. 'I have to get up early tomorrow morning. I have an important appointment.'

Stephanie felt her cheeks burn and his smile mocked her, reminded her, warned her not to forget to keep that appointment.

'Oh, this wasn't just a pleasure trip, then? You have business in the town? Legal business, I suppose—I hadn't heard of any exciting legal developments in Wyville.'

'This is . . .' Gerard paused, his face bland, then said, 'more personal than legal.'

Euan laughed. 'Sorry I asked. Then you mustn't keep the lady waiting, must you?'

'I hope she won't keep me waiting,' drawled Gerard. As he turned to go his eyes flickered over Stephanie's face, hardening. Then he was gone and the anxious fire inside her died down, leaving her in a state of weary misery. Robert and Euan noticed; they insisted that she must go home to bed. They went on to the Laserlight club without her to meet Gwen. All the younger people at the party went in a big group to dance and drink for several hours; it was the latest 'in' place in Wyville. Stephanie was relieved not to have to endure the chatter and brash music, the darkness split by sudden violent colours as the laser lights cut through the room. She wouldn't have enjoyed it tonight; she needed to be alone to think. She went to bed and lay in the dark, her mind pursuing the past and wondering what Gerard Tenniel was going to say to her tomorrow.

She had to go; there was no escape. He knew that; his eyes had stressed the weakness of her own position. He had the whip hand and he would use it ruthlessly if she didn't fall into line.

But why did he want to talk to her? What was there to talk about? She stared at the ceiling, watching the moon make delicate lace patterns on the plaster. From time to time the headlights of a car cut across the room, making her blink. Robert and Gwen would be home soon; it was nearly one o'clock. They never stayed out too late. Their lives were too dedicated. So was Euan's; he was totally devoted to his career, to his patients.

She had been living in a fool's paradise, imagining that she could ever marry Euan. Her background made that impossible. Why hadn't she seen that? Why hadn't Robert said something? He must have known; it must have dawned on him that if anything ever came out about what had happened five years ago there would be a scandal which would make life unlivable for her here.

She closed her eyes and tried to sleep. She had to get up at first light and drive back to the hotel. She would try to slip in without being noticed. Nobody must see her going up to Gerard Tenniel's room.

She heard her brother and his wife drive up, the quiet sound of their front door closing. At least she wouldn't have to sneak out tomorrow past their door, she had her own exit. They would sleep late, they wouldn't hear her. If only she could get to sleep! She was going to be exhausted in the morning.

Perhaps Gerard Tenniel wanted to find out if she was genuinely in love with Euan. Perhaps if he believed she was, he wouldn't tell them anything.

She mustn't harbour wild hopes; he was capable of utter ruthlessness. She turned over, thumping her pillow. She wouldn't think about him any more: tomorrow would come soon enough and she would find out then what was in that tortuous mind of his.

She woke up in the morning with a shuddering start when her alarm went off at six-thirty. For a few seconds she was dazed; wondering why her head banged like a tin drum. Then she remembered and swung out of bed, staggering a little as she went to the bathroom.

She had thought out a plan last night, a way of appearing at the hotel at that early hour without arousing too much surprise.

She showered and combed her hair and dressed in her pastel-pink tracksuit. If she turned up at the hotel saying she had been jogging and wanted to shower and change before she went home her excuse might be accepted.

She let herself out of the house very quietly and drove away, parking on the deserted sea front. She jogged for ten minutes until she felt herself beginning to perspire, then began to run towards the hotel.

The night staff looked up as she came into the

reception lobby. 'Hallo, Stevie—don't tell me you've been up all night?' asked the night desk clerk, grinning at her, then he let his eyes move over her tracksuit. 'You must have energy to burn! I thought you went to a party last night?'

'I did but I had a headache and I thought a little fresh air might clear my head.' She leaned on the desk, breathing heavily. 'Mind if I have a shower and change before I drive home? I'll use one of the bathrooms upstairs, I don't suppose any of the guests will be stirring.' She had brought along a small zip-topped bag in which she had put a change of clothes; she waved it at the night clerk. 'Okay by you?'

'Be my guest,' he laughed and watched her walk unsteadily over to the lift. 'You poor dear, you're hardly able to move a muscle. Want me to come and scrub your back for you?'

Stephanie pretended to laugh as she stepped into the waiting lift. Alone and unseen, her face lapsed into lines of anxiety. She had got over hurdle number one. While she was idly chatting to the desk clerk she had been able to run her eye over the guest book to check which room they had given Gerard Tenniel. Now all she had to do was get inside his room without being seen.

She left the lift at his floor and hovered, glancing around to make sure the coast was clear, then walked quickly to his door and tapped softly.

There was a pause during which Stephanie was on tenterhooks in case someone came out of one of the other rooms, or a member of the staff came up with a breakfast tray for a guest. She was so nervous that when the door did open she hurried into the room without looking at Gerard. Only when he closed the door and leant on it, watching her ironically, did she look round at him.

Her first glimpse was a shock. He wasn't dressed. He was only wearing a short white towelling robe beneath which he was obviously naked. He looked as if he had just had a bath, his blond hair damp, darkened by water, clinging to his scalp, emphasising the razor-edged lines of his face. Stephanie's nervous eyes ran over him and up to his face again.

'Please say what you have to say quickly. I have to get back before I'm missed,' she said flatly.

'What did you tell your family?' Gerard observed her speculatively. 'That you were going out jogging?' His mouth twisted. 'You're good at telling lies.'

Heat burned in her face. 'I didn't tell them anything. I have a flat of my own. I didn't need to explain where I was going, they aren't up yet.'

'Last night I gathered that you lived with your brother and his wife.'

'My flat is over their garage.'

He nodded coolly. 'I see. And your parents? Where are they now?'

She looked away. 'My father died a year ago. My mother is still in Australia, she liked it there, and my sister and her family are nearby, so . . .' She broke off, sighing. 'Can we get to the point? I want to get this over with.'

He turned his head towards the door, his eyes alert. 'That must be Room Service bringing my breakfast. You'd better go into the bathroom, unless of course you don't mind the waiter seeing you here?'

She hated him; hated the mockery and sarcasm in his voice, the way the grey eyes watched her stiffen and understood her alarm. Did it give him pleasure to torture her, play with her like a cat with a mouse?

She could hear the rattle of crockery on the table which the waiter was wheeling along the corridor now. Silently she walked across the room and bolted herself into the bathroom. While she was in here she might as well shower again and dress. She had to keep up the pretence that that was why she was here—she could hardly leave the hotel still wearing her tracksuit.

She stripped off, hearing the tap on the door. 'Room Service, sir! Your breakfast.'

Stephanie ran the shower and stepped under it; tensing as the cool needles of water touched her hot skin. She couldn't hear voices in the room beyond while the water was running. It was a rapid shower, then she stepped out again and began to towel herself angrily. She had brought a neat grey skirt and blue blouse in her bag; she hurriedly dressed in them and spent two minutes combing her hair, putting on a pink lipstick and powdering her nose.

'Are you staying in there all day?' Gerard's voice enquired drily on the other side of the door.

Stephanie unbolted it and pulled it open. He surveyed her with a faint curiosity, his pale brows lifting.

'That was quick.' His gaze sauntered down over her from her head to her feet. 'Very demure.'

She walked past him, ignoring the trace of acid in his tone. The breakfast table had been set up near the window, which had been opened, so that sunshine flooded in and a faint spring breeze brought the salt smell and soft whispering of the sea. It was an idyllic scene: the table was covered with white damask, a yellow rose in a small glass vase standing among the covered dishes and coffee-pots.

'I ordered breakfast for two,' Gerard told her as she stared at the table. 'Room Service were discreetly curious as this is a single suite, but they were far too well-mannered to query it. I took the liberty of ordering a continental breakfast for you: orange juice, croissants and coffee. I hope that was a good guess.'

'I'm not hungry, thanks.'

'After all that jogging?' he mocked. 'Of course you are. Sit down.'

'No, thank you.'

He came up behind her, his hands grasping her slender shoulders, and forced her down into a chair as if she was a child.

Before she could get up again he leaned over and placed the glass of orange juice in front of her. 'Coffee?' He picked up the heavy silver pot and poured some coffee into her cup. 'Cream? No, you still drink it black? No sugar, either, I seem to remember.'

Her agonised eyes shot up to his face and he smiled tightly. 'I have a very good memory. I never forget an important detail, a vital part of my professional training.'

There was no point in pleading with him, begging him to get this over with, deliver his blow and let her stumble away. He would play this his way and her plea would merely increase his enjoyment of having her at his mercy. He never forgot—and he never forgave. She hadn't known him very long, five years ago, but she had learnt that much about him. Gerard Tenniel was a hard man.

With a shaky hand she picked up her glass of orange juice which was served, as the hotel always served it, embedded in a silver goblet of crushed ice, the way their chef had learnt to serve orange juice when he

worked in America for some years. The hotel was very
lucky to have Joe; he was an excellent head chef and
could have got a job in any of the luxury London
hotels, but had chosen to come back to Wyville to be
near his ageing mother who refused to move from her
home of many years.

'You've changed,' Gerard observed thoughtfully as
he sat down opposite her and took the cover off his
own orange juice. 'Five years is a long time, of course,
and you were only eighteen, weren't you?'

Stephanie's blue eyes stayed on his hard-boned face.
He said that so coolly, but had he ever stopped to
consider what he was saying? She had been eighteen,
still half a child. Far too young to know how to cope
with the nightmare situation which suddenly exploded
around her.

'I've often wondered what became of you. I knew
you'd left Australia, but I had no idea you had come to
Wyville. An odd coincidence. If my mother hadn't
had a letter from Margo Cameron I'd never have
found out where you were.' Gerard had sipped some of
his juice; now he took the cover off a dish of scrambled
egg and tomatoes and began to eat them with a fork.

Stephanie found it hard to swallow. She pushed her
own juice to one side and took a croissant and broke it
into little pieces. It gave her trembling fingers
something to do. Gerard's eyes lifted, observed what
she was doing, his mouth twisting.

'Eat something. You look as if you need the blood
sugar.'

'You may be enjoying this, but I'm not,' she broke
out, her voice hoarse. 'Please Mr Tenniel ...'

'Mr Tenniel?' he repeated with barbed irony. 'You
used to call me Gerard.'

Her pallor became a scalding rush of hot blood and she looked down again. She heard him laugh and felt like throwing her cup of coffee at him. How could he sit there, calmly eating scrambled egg, buttering toast, drinking coffee, while she waited like a convicted criminal to hear her sentence?

'Or don't you remember that?' he mocked.

She didn't even bother to answer. There was no point—it had been a purely rhetorical question, he knew she hadn't forgotten him or their brief relationship before the nightmare started. All this was part of his deliberate torture; he had learnt this slow needling technique years ago when he was training for the bar, no doubt. It worked with witnesses who had something to hide; he was a very successful barrister now. She had occasionally seen his name in newspaper reports of cases and had known that he was back in England—but then at the time he had told her that he was only in Australia for a year on a sabbatical course to study the Australian legal system. She had realised that he would come back to England, too, but he was an ambitious man and a clever lawyer and she had guessed that he would aim for London and get a place in a good chambers there. Their paths had been very unlikely to cross. She had felt safe here in Wyville; it was such a tranquil backwater. She had blithely imagined that Gerard Tenniel could have no connections there, but she had been wrong.

He had finished his breakfast and was leaning back in his chair with his second cup of coffee, studying her with narrowed eyes.

She sat up, too, tensed for the attack, her hands clenched in her lap. She hadn't eaten a thing and had only had a few sips of orange juice. Her coffee was cold; she couldn't bring herself to drink any of it.

Gerard smiled and said calmly, 'Euan doesn't know, does he?'

She didn't answer even then. Anything she said would be used against her.

'And when I tell him, he won't want to know you,' Gerard added, after waiting to see how she would react.

'And you *are* going to tell him!' Stephanie muttered harshly. 'I'm surprised you waited. Why not tell him last night? But then you couldn't have had the fun of playing cat and mouse with me if you had, could you? You didn't want to miss out on that. It's made your day, hasn't it, sitting here laughing at me, sticking your poisoned needles into me, making me wait and suffer, when all the time you knew you were going to tell Euan anyway. I should never have come, I shouldn't have let you put me through this.'

He was staring at her, his face taut, his mouth a straight line. She would never have spoken to him like that five years ago, she had been too shy, too awed by him. Every time he turned those mocking grey eyes on her she had blushed and felt dizzy. She had thought she was in love, but she had been too young to know what love was or she would have realised that Gerard Tenniel was only amusing himself by flirting with her. His eyes had smiled, then, though; they had almost had a tenderness in them. Now they were sharp, cold flint.

'But you did come,' he said through those tight, contemptuous lips, the words a mere thread of sound holding a faint question.

Stephanie answered the question he hadn't asked. 'Not for myself, I didn't come here to plead for myself—I can't stop you telling Euan and his mother, and you're probably right, that will be the end of everything between us then. Euan wouldn't want a wife who'd been mixed up in anything like a murder trial. But none of that matters as much as what this would do to my brother, to Robert. He's a doctor, at the hospital, and it would ruin his life here, wreck his reputation—he might be asked to leave and he likes it here, he'll be shattered if that happens.' She got up, her hands gripping the back of the chair, her face set and white. 'You can't do that to him. I'll go away. I won't marry Euan, I'll never see him again, but please . . . please, promise me you won't tell the Camerons, or anyone here in Wyville.'

CHAPTER THREE

GERARD TENNIEL considered her, one long-fingered hand tapping idly on the edge of his chair. Stephanie waited, hardly breathing, for his answer. Surely he couldn't refuse her? If he went ahead and broke this story it would be so cruelly unfair to Robert and Gwen. He might hate her, but he had no grudge against her brother.

'You say you wouldn't marry Cameron, you'd leave town and not come back?'

She nodded, a heaviness oppressing her at the very prospect.

'How do I know you'd keep your word?' His smile iced her blood; it held such cynicism and contempt. 'We both know what a liar you are—and a cheat. What if you waited a few weeks until I was out of the way and then came back and took up with Cameron again?'

'I wouldn't do that!'

'How do I know that? He's loaded, isn't he? A very eligible bachelor who could give you everything that greedy little mind of yours has always been after.'

She flinched. 'That isn't true! I'm not like that; you have no right to say such things. I'm not interested in Euan's money, I like him for himself.'

He laughed in derision. 'Do you expect me to believe that? You were always interested in money. Why else did you encourage Burgess? A man twice your age, going bald, with the personality of a white

45

rabbit—but he had money, didn't he? He had position, status, a beautiful house, even a yacht. What did it matter to you that he was forty years old to your eighteen? Or that he had a wife already?'

Stephanie's head drooped on that long, slim neck, the sun picking out streaks of gold among the dark brown hair, gilt tips on the thick lashes clustering on her cheek. The man seated at the table watched her, his mouth reined tightly, a slight tic beating beside it, as though he was not quite as in control of himself as he wanted her to believe. The grey eyes blazed with some emotion; rage or distaste, perhaps, or something in which those feelings mingled.

'I can't argue with you, you wouldn't listen to me, just as nobody would at the time, nobody believed me, but I'd done nothing to encourage Theo Burgess. Nothing. I was sorry for him, that was all. It wasn't my fault if . . .'

'You can save your breath. I don't want to hear a speech for the defence from you. We'll take it that you would like me to think you were innocent, but whether you were or not, I know one thing for certain—Margo Cameron wouldn't want you married to her son, part of the family.' Gerard got up slowly, his long, powerful body moving without haste towards her. 'I'll also admit that I have no wish to wreck your brother's life. I imagine he went through enough five years ago. He was still a medical student then, wasn't he? I seem to remember you telling me that he was in his last year at one of the London teaching hospitals.'

Stephanie nodded wearily. His memory was perfect, he had forgotten nothing.

'It must have been tough on him, having to take his final exams just when his sister was involved in a public scandal. I wouldn't want to drag it all up again, but on the other hand, Margo Cameron is my godmother. I couldn't keep silent and let you go ahead and marry her son. She would never forgive me.'

'I've said I'll go away, what more do you want?' she burst out bitterly, her eyes lifting and watching him with bitter hostility. 'Oh, why did you have to come here? I was happy again. I thought I'd forgotten it all, put it behind me, and then you turn up and . . .'

She dropped her head into her hands to hide the tears helplessly welling up in her blue eyes. She wouldn't cry in front of him. He wasn't going to have the pleasure of seeing her break down. Five years ago she had stood in a witness box giving evidence, while from the well of the court Gerard's savage eyes watched her—hated her. It was like being watched from hiding by some wild animal tracking you to pull you down and tear you to pieces.

She had been stricken when she heard that the firm he was attached to for a year had taken Viola's case; she knew it meant that Gerard would be in court. She hadn't seen him throughout the long months before the case was finally given a date for a hearing. It had been nerve-racking enough to face the trial itself; having to face Gerard too made it so much worse.

She had made mistakes, stammered, tried desperately to avoid meeting his eyes. She must have looked the picture of guilt; the evidence was so damning. She hadn't expected that Gerard would stare at her with such crushing contempt, though. She had had to fight for self-control during the hours when she was in the box; first giving her evidence, then under cross-examination followed by a re-examination by the prosecution lawyer who was intent on trying to underline the points in her story which the defence lawyers had tried to destroy. All the time Gerard had watched her from the defence bench with a bitter hostility, and that had been the part of her ordeal which was least tolerable.

She rubbed a hand over her wet eyes. She hadn't broken down in front of him then; she wouldn't now.

He was closer than she had expected; standing right beside her, his face harsh. 'Tears won't work with me, Stephanie.'

'I'm not crying,' she said huskily.

He put out a hand; his finger touched her wet lashes, brushing over them, making her jump. Incredulously, she saw him lick his finger, tasting her tears.

'Real tears,' he said tersely, as she stared, shocked by the strangeness of the little action.

'Are you glad about that?' she asked, close to hysteria. 'Did you want to make me cry? I'm sorry I didn't weep buckets for you. Maybe if you hit me I might—you haven't tried that yet. You've insulted me, threatened me, talked to me as if I was below contempt—what comes next? What do you want to do to me?'

'Don't tempt me,' he said, and with disbelief she saw him laugh; a humourless laughter, low and harsh. 'I thought you were such a little innocent; eighteen, never been kissed, big blue eyes like a baby, skin like a peach—God, I thought you were beautiful, and so sweet. I hardly dared touch you with a finger in case you went into panic or in case I lost my head and went out of control, because I wanted you, Stephanie, I wanted you like hell, but I wouldn't risk scaring you and so I made myself hold off, treat you carefully, when all the time you were letting that bald old man . . .'

His voice broke off in a guttural snarl. 'God! You made a fool of me!' The grey eyes swept over her, the hard mouth taut.

Stephanie was whiter than ever, her blue eyes very dark and enormous with shock and emotion. She put out a hand to him, her mouth trembling.

'Gerard, if you liked me then, don't do this to me now. Don't hurt my brother through me! I'll do anything not to hurt him.'

He took her hand, held it. Stared down at it oddly, as if he had never seen a hand before, turning it palm upwards as if he might be going to read her lifeline, her future, predict what else lay in store for her.

'Is this a proposition,' he asked in a low, husky voice.

Stiffening, she tried to pull her hand free, but he would not release it. He slid his fingers underneath hers, still holding her firmly, his eyes still fixed on her palm.

'I might be prepared to do a deal,' he murmured, and she gave a gasp of shock.

'What . . . what are you talking about?'

'You know what I'm talking about.' He slowly bent his head and Stephanie shivered with a terrifying mixture of excitement and horror; her mouth went dry, her skin turned icy and then burned.

Gerard's mouth touched her palm and and her eyes closed; she swayed, shuddering. It was the strangest kiss she had ever had in her life: his lips had a strangely deep heat, and suddenly she remembered a moment five years when they were dancing together at a party at the Burgesses' house and Gerard had taken her out into the garden to show her the Australian moon, copper-coloured, rising through mists in that echoing vault of a sky. There had been music from the house and a constant noise of insects, cicadas or crickets. It had been so hot; she had fanned herself with a fern branch and listened while he pointed out the stars, naming them. She had been breathless, enthralled, watching his handsome profile and that silken blond head, her heart beating so fast it made her giddy. And then Gerard had looked down at her and smiled, and he had kissed her hand the way he was doing now: slowly, with intense passion and a sensuality that turned her knees to water.

He lifted his head and their eyes met, and she came back to this moment, to the present—and the bitter knowledge that the way he had just kissed her hand had not been the same at all. Just now there had been an insulting quality to that kiss, something that had not been present that first time.

'I'll hold my tongue, Stephanie,' he said softly, watching her. 'On one condition.'

She didn't move, didn't ask what he meant—his grey eyes were eloquent enough, she knew what he was going to say before he said it, and her whole body went rigid with denial, with refusal, with hatred.

'I still want you,' he said, smiling.

Stephanie had never thought that a smile could hurt so much. He used it like a poniard, stabbing her, watching intently to see her bleed.

'Perhaps even more now,' he added, enjoying her helpless rejection, the look in the blue eyes. 'Ironic, really—I'd put you on a pedestal, I was just at the age when a very young, very innocent girl could get to me, really get to me. I wanted to strew rose-petals for you to walk on; I was head over heels in romantic dreams about you. My last madness, I suppose. I was thirty-two and I'd had all the fun of finding out about women; all that was over and I was thinking of settling down, getting married. When I was in my teens I chased the glamorous types: experienced women much older than myself. Most boys of eighteen are turned on by women who know what sex is all about, and I was no exception. I didn't even bother to look at girls of my own age; they bored me stiff. Innocence was something I wanted to shed as fast as I could. But by the time I'd met you I'd gone full circle. I was sick of women who were ready to jump into bed at one word from a man. I knew I would only marry a girl who'd never known any other man.'

'My God . . .' Stephanie was still trembling, but anger was burning up inside her. 'Talk about double standards, you're a hypocrite, a total hypocrite—one law for you, another for women, is that it?'

He smiled drily. 'That's it. Maybe it is a double standard. It was what I felt then—I wanted . . .' He broke off, his teeth biting down on his lower lip, and was silent for almost a minute, staring at her.

'Well, never mind. I've told you the deal I'm offering. It's up to you to decide whether to come away with me and leave your brother to carry on with his life here in peace—or to stay and take the consequences.'

She turned and walked away shakily towards the window. The town was coming to life; the sun glittered on the pale waves she could see between the buildings along the sea front. There was far more traffic now. She would have to leave soon or Robert and Gwen would wonder what on earth had happened to her, and she was in no state to face their questions.

She leaned on the windowsill, grateful for the support. 'You know this is blackmail, don't you?' she accused.

'Call it what you like, but make up your mind before tomorrow. Whatever happens, you won't be marrying Euan Cameron, get that through your head.' Gerard paused and she felt his eyes fixed on her back; they burned through the thin material of her blouse like a red-hot laser.

'Are you in love with him?' The grate of his voice made her nerves jangle.

'That's no business of yours!' she snapped, and for a moment there was silence in the room. A seagull flew past the window, sunlight striking the underside of the spread white wings, turning them to magical molten gold so that the bird had a new beauty. On any other day Stephanie would have been entranced by that; her spirits lifted, her mind illuminated by that glimpse of fleeting beauty. Today her eye dully followed the gull's flight while she tried to think.

What was she to do? Gerard was offering her a choice between her own happiness and Robert's, or was it even that simple? She wasn't going to be happy whatever choice she made. He was right about that. Euan wouldn't marry her now. She couldn't marry him even if he swore he didn't care about the scandal attached to her. Gerard Tenniel's arrival had made that much crystal clear to her. She should have known it without needing him to point it out, but she had been kidding herself, allowing herself to dream impossible dreams.

She would have to go away. How could she explain to Euan that she suddenly did not want to see him any more? Everyone expected them to get married; they were too close to make an abrupt separation possible without some explanation. Even if she tried to break off with him, Euan wouldn't let it go at that. He would demand to know what was behind her change of heart and he wasn't the type to be convinced by some glib fabrication. He was too shrewd, too tough-minded. No, she would have to leave town without a word. Euan would be hurt, he would try to find her. Robert would be baffled and upset too. All her friends would be stunned.

She would have to go, but she certainly wasn't leaving with Gerard. Did he really think that she would let herself be blackmailed into bed with him? She closed her eyes, sickness clawing at her. The very idea of giving herself to him, knowing he despised her, knowing that the price of his silence had been her body, made her feel unclean.

She turned slowly, her mind made up. 'I have until tomorrow, then?' she asked in a remote, cold voice.

He was watching her with narrowed eyes, the sunlight falling on his beautifully sculpted face. She remembered so vividly how his bone structure ran: the high, austere cheekbones and the strength of jaw and temples. She had often stared at him and been struck dumb with wonder by that combination of fair hair and lean vitality.

'What's going on inside that head, I wonder?' he asked, rubbing one thumb along his jaw, his expression thoughtful. 'I hope you aren't planning anything I wouldn't like. I wouldn't advise you to try skipping town without telling me.' His quick eyes caught the flicker of apprehension in her face and he gave a silky little sound. 'Aha! I see you were planning just that.' His smile was menacing. 'It wouldn't do you any good,

Stephanie. I'd feel that you'd broken our agreement and I'd be forced to tell the Camerons everything.'

'You really are a bastard, aren't you?' she whispered.

'I mean what I say—if that's being a bastard. We have a deal or we don't. If you don't keep your side of the bargain, why should I keep mine?'

'I don't see what you'll get out of this—I'll hate you, can't you see that?' she burst out, and he moved towards her, smiling.

'How do you think I felt about you five years ago when I discovered that the blue-eyed innocent I'd been treating with such reverence was just a little whore?'

The last word didn't quite leave his lips. In the middle of it she hit him; so hard that his head snapped back and a dark red stain came up in his cheek.

Only as she saw the livid flash of his eyes did she realise what she had done. Her palm stung, she watched him with fear, thinking for a moment that he was going to hit her back. The violence between them had a tangible quality; the air burned with it.

Then he swung away, his back to her, as if he couldn't trust himself if he faced her. She sensed that he was fighting to get control of himself; it was a minute before he turned round again and by then the dark stain on his cheek was beginning to fade.

The look in his eyes made her shrink. 'You shouldn't have done that, Stephanie,' he said very softly. 'I won't forget it.'

She hurriedly moved to the door, picking up her bag, in which she had stuffed her tracksuit and running shoes.

'I must go or Robert and Gwen will wonder . . .'

'You have a car, don't you?'

She nodded, her hand on the door.

'Good. I came by train because I wanted to be certain of getting here early enough for the party and driving would have taken too long. We can use your car to go back to London, though.'

'My car? But . . .'

'Be here at nine tomorrow,' he interrupted, ignoring her angry protest.

She made one last attempt to make him be reasonable. 'You can't be serious about this. You can't mean it. It's crazy!'

He laughed. 'Crazy? Yes, perhaps. But I mean it, Stephanie, don't think for one second that I don't.'

She ran a shaky hand over her face, rubbing her eyes, as though she thought she was having a bad dream and would wake up any minute.

'Look, be reasonable, Gerard—I understand why you can't let me marry Euan. I was stupid to think I could; I don't want to hurt the Camerons by involving them in an old scandal. But to blackmail me like this! How can you do it? *Why* are you doing it?'

The grey eyes glittered, she saw his nostrils flare. 'You aren't that naïve!' He ran a finger lightly down her throat and she flinched as though he had hit her. 'Let's say I have an old obsession to satisfy—or an unpaid bill to collect. You used me ruthlessly as cover for your affair with Burgess . . .'

'No, that isn't true!'

He ignored her outcry. 'And in my turn I'm using you. That's fair, isn't it?'

Stephanie closed her eyes briefly, then gave a deep, painful sigh. He was crazy. He was out of his mind. But she was in his power and there was nothing she could do about it without hurting people she loved.

'I can't just walk out at a moment's notice, though. What about my job?'

'With unemployment as high as I gather it is here, they won't have any problem in getting a replacement at once.'

She tried another argument desperately. 'But my brother—what shall I tell him? You aren't thinking straight, Gerard. People don't pack up and leave home without a good reason. My brother is my landlord, too. What about my flat? All my things here? Robert is bound to ask questions, want to know where I'm going and why?'

'You'll think of something.' His smile was cynical, mocking. 'You're very inventive.'

'Damn you!' she whispered, staring at him. Why was he smiling as though she had paid him a compliment?

'Tell him you've fallen madly in love with me and we're going to live together,' he suggested, and she flushed darkly.

'He wouldn't believe me; he knows I'm not the type.'

'He obviously doesn't know you very well. Or does he know you better than I think? Tell him I'm rich and can give you the earth. That will convince him.'

She sighed wearily. 'Gerard, listen . . .' She put a hand on his arm and he glanced down at it, lids hooded. 'Gerard, tell me the truth—are you playing games with me? Is this some sort of prolonged teasing? Five years is such a long time. You can't have carried a grudge against me all those years. My God, I'd almost forgotten your name!'

She shouldn't have said that. The grey eyes held a

seething violence; his mouth hardened and tensed.

'Then you'll never forget it again! You have just one choice—so I'd advise you to be here precisely at nine o'clock tomorrow.'

He pulled open the door and she slowly walked out of the room, turning with another cry of protest: 'Gerard, I . . .'

He shut the door on her and she stared dumbly at the polished wooden panels. This could not be happening. He couldn't mean it. He was a barrister, for heaven's sake; he lived by the law, he understood it. He was supposed to uphold it. Yet he was cold-bloodedly blackmailing her into giving herself to him to buy his silence.

What if she went to the police? He would end up in prison. She began to walk slowly along the carpeted corridor towards the lifts.

He wouldn't, of course. What evidence did she have? Would the police believe her story? She was the one who had been mixed up in an unsavoury court case five years ago. If the police investigated her background they would soon uncover the details of the murder trial; the accusations against her, the reputation she had acquired during that trial.

Gerard was a well known, very successful, very respectable barrister.

Which of them would the police believe? If she did attempt to tell her story all she would achieve was that her secret would be known to the whole town, Robert would have to give up his job and move, Euan and his family would find themselves engulfed by scandal and she would carry the blame for all that.

When Stephanie emerged from the ground floor she was lucky enough to be swept out of the hotel in a tide of guests heading for a waiting coach. The desk clerk was too busy to notice her. She walked along the sea front to her car, staring at the sunlit tide pouring on to the sand. It was going to be a fine day; the sky was blue and the waves reflected that deep colour.

What in heaven's name was she going to tell Robert and Gwen? She couldn't discuss it with them face to face—she simply couldn't lie and then have to answer questions . . . and there *would* be startled, worried questions!

It took her ten minutes to drive back and to her relief she realised that her brother and his wife weren't yet up. Their bedroom curtains were still closed. They would be sleeping late after last night.

Stephanie slipped into her own flat and sat down to think the problem out, but she could see no way round it. She would have to write Robert and Gwen a letter. Gerard was right—the only thing she could do was tell her brother that she had fallen in love and was going away with Gerard. Euan was going to be badly hurt. Her eyes clouded with tears. What on earth would he think of her? But however low his opinion after reading her letter, he would have thought far worse if he ever heard about the Burgess case and her involvement in it.

Was that going to overshadow her whole life? She had only just left school when her parents decided to take her out to Australia with them to visit her married sister who had been living there for four years. Stephanie had been over the moon. She hadn't been further than France until then and suddenly she was flying right the way round the world, stopping off at exotic and exciting places whose very names were like a string of flashing stones: Singapore, Bali,

Bangkok, Hong Kong. It was the trip of a lifetime and her parents knew it would never be repeated. They meant to stay in Australia for at least a year, possibly longer, but as they were on that side of the world it seemed silly to miss the chance of visiting other places which had only been names on a map until they had the opportunity of spending a few days at each.

Their travel agent had worked out a travelling schedule and booked hotels and flights. The Stuarts planned the trip for months ahead, arguing over where to stop off, how long to spend at each place. They couldn't leave until Stephanie had finished her summer exams and was free to go with them. Robert was going to be working through the summer; he had a temporary job in a holiday camp. He no longer lived at home by then: he had digs in a hostel near his London hospital, so the Stuarts didn't have to worry about him.

It wasn't until they finally reached Australia that it dawned on them that Stephanie's presence would create a problem for their daughter and son-in-law. Andrea was delighted to see her sister, who had been a little girl the last time they met, but her bungalow only had three bedrooms. She and her husband shared one with their youngest, the baby, Benny; the second room was fully occupied by Andrea's three-year-old twin girls, Ann and Philippa, and the third room was earmarked for the Stuart parents.

'You don't mind sleeping on the couch in the living-room, do you, Stevie?' Andrea asked uncertainly and, of course, Stephanie said she'd be perfectly comfortable doing that, but she could see that in the constricted space of the bungalow, which had only one big room apart from the three small bedrooms, it made

life awkward for her sister to have her using the couch
as a bed. Phil had to get up at the crack of dawn to go
to work. If he forgot something he needed, left it in the
living-room the night before, he had to tiptoe through
the darkened room, stumbling over chairs, in search of
whatever he wanted.

Stephanie didn't say anything to her parents; she
simply made up her mind that she must get a job and
somewhere else to live. She couldn't occupy the couch
in the living-room for a whole year, but if she said she
wanted to go back to England, her parents would feel
they had to come too. They wouldn't like the idea of
her living alone on the other side of the world from
them.

She began reading the small ads in papers and
almost at once found what she wanted—a job as a
mother's help on a farm in Queensland, only fifty
miles from Andrea's home. She would have her own
room and full board and be earning a real salary for
the firt time in her life. She showed it to her parents,
who agreed that she could apply, and a few days later
her brother-in-law drove her to the Burgess house for
an interview with Mrs Burgess.

Stephanie had liked her at first. It was hard to
believe that now, but she had soon come to realise that
Mrs Burgess could put on an act which deceived
almost everyone she met. She wasn't so much two-
faced as a dual personality.

Stephanie was shown around the beautiful, luxuri-
ously furnished house and grounds which stretched
further than you could see from the upper-storey
windows. She was bowled over by the beauty of the
place. Mrs Burgess was delighted by the wide-eyed
amazement, and she offered Stephanie the job.

There were two Burgess children, five-year-old Matt and seven-year-old Elnora. Even at that first meeting, Stephanie sensed something odd about them. They were quiet and well behaved, but seemed very nervous, especially with their mother. Stephanie had been naïve enough to decide that Mrs Burgess must be very strict with them.

On that first visit she did not meet Theo Burgess; his wife had said that he was away on business. She had made it clear that her husband was a wealthy man: he owned several large farms and a canning factory, and was a prominent member of local society.

Mrs Burgess was a very beautiful woman: in her late twenties, she managed to look far younger, her skin smooth and suntanned, her eyes the colour of jade, a cool green, her hair blonde and bleached almost white by hours of sunbathing every day. She dressed with flair; it was obvious that her husband gave her anything she wanted, for her slim wrists were loaded with bracelets, her fingers with rings that flashed as she talked.

Even at that first meeting, though, there were reservations in Stephanie's mind about her. Even Phil had commented, as he drove her back to his home, 'Did you ever see so much expensive junk on a woman? I'm surprised she could walk with all those stones weighing her down!'

'She was wearing a lot of jewellery,' Stephanie agreed doubtfully.

'A lot? Honey, she jingled with it! A lot of money and no taste. Well, who cares? So long as she treats you right she can wear the Taj Mahal on her head as far as I'm concerned.' He had grinned round at her, white teeth gleaming. Phil was an Australian of two generations, although he was descended from English settlers. It was while he was back in England in search of his ancestors that he had met Andrea and fallen in love. Andrea still had to be careful how much time she spent in the sun at one time, but Phil soaked it up, his skin had inherited tan from the day he was born, Stephanie suspected. He had been brown and glowing even in London after weeks away from his native land.

'Are you sure you'll be okay there?' Andrea had asked her that evening, looking anxious. 'Fifty miles isn't far out here, but it may seem like it to you at first. But if you need us, just pick up that phone and we'll come and get you.'

Stephanie had been slightly nervous, of course, but on her first day at Sweetwater she had met Theo Burgess and been reassured by his gentleness and calm manner. He was, as Gerard had unpleasantly pointed out, old enough to be her father—a man just over forty, inclined to be a little overweight, his hair receding and turning grey.

He seemed slightly uneasy about Stephanie's age. 'You're younger than I'd expected, are you sure you can cope? My children are in need of firm handling.'

'They seemed very well mannered, I'm sure I will get on with them, and your wife is charming.'

She had expected him to smile at that, but she saw anxiety in his pale eyes, which surprised and bothered her. Why did he look at her like that?

He had sighed, giving a little shrug. 'Well, we'll see how things go.'

Stephanie had been depressed by that interview in one way. She realised that her job was far from secure. But on the other hand she liked Mr Burgess: he had been the unknown quantity involved in the job, or so she imagined! Having met him she now knew she had nothing to worry about from him; all Andrea's lectures about how to react if her boss tried to make a pass at her could be forgotten.

A week later she had met Gerard Tenniel at dinner. He was a remote cousin of Mrs Burgess, a young barrister spending a year in Australia as part of an exchange scheme. He was acting as a junior in a well-known set of chambers, going around the circuit with his senior counsel, learning how the Australian legal system worked and earning his keep by doing whatever work the head of chambers set aside for him, largely briefs which paid little and were just good experience.

That evening he hardly took his eyes off Stephanie and after dinner cornered her on the terrace where she was watching the stars and asked her out to dinner the next day.

Stephanie was barely eighteen; he scared and excited her. He was the most beautiful man she had ever seen: above his dark evening clothes his fair head gleamed like pale silk; his skin had acquired a golden tan, his grey eyes were mysterious and inviting. He turned her head, right from the start, and she didn't know how to talk to him—she just sat and listened, chin in hand, while Gerard talked. She had promised to write to her best friend at school who had gone on to university in Bristol, and her letters to Liz were soon full of nothing but Gerard. Liz obviously didn't believe the half of it. She bluntly said so, teasing Stephanie about her wild imagination, so Stephanie sent her photographs of herself and Gerard, swimming, dancing, sunbathing.

She was so wrapped up in Gerard that it was quite a while before it dawned on her that Mrs Burgess no longer liked her. Gradually she noticed other things—that her employer's wife was changeable, erratic, moody—one minute sunny and smiling, and the next becoming violent or malicious or even both. Stephanie slowly realised why Matt and Elnora were nervous of their mother—they never knew where they were with her. She hugged and kissed them one minute, calling them her precious pets; the next she slapped them viciously, once even drawing blood from a cut made by one of her rings on Elnora's cheek.

Stephanie found herself watching them, trying never to leave them alone with their mother. She only went out with Gerard if they could go with her during the day. At night she knew that their father would be around so it was safe to see Gerard in the evenings.

Theo Burgess didn't confide in her at once. He was a very discreet man, intelligent, cautious, self-contained. It was after the incident when his wife made Elnora's face bleed, that Theo first hinted that his wife wasn't quite normal, and even then he tried to wrap it up in muffling words, veil it, in case he frightened Stephanie too much.

'My wife is highly strung and she has a quick temper, it's better not to let the children see too much of her, sometimes they get on her nerves and . . .' He smiled uneasily. 'Well, you know how mothers can be at certain times; a little edgy. You will be careful with the children, Miss Stuart?'

Some afternoons he took time off work to swim with his children and he and Stephanie played games with them, throwing rubber rings from one to the other, having a water-polo match in the pool with lilos for horses and a big beach-ball they smacked with the flat of their hands. They were noisy, uninhibited games; they all behaved like children, splashing and shouting and laughing, and very soon Theo was calling her Stevie, the way the children did.

He was an utterly devoted father; he loved both Matt and Elnora equally and had their love in return. Seeing them when they were so happy together, when Viola Burgess was absent, finally made Stephanie realise that there was something very wrong with her employer's wife.

Viola had maids to do the housework, of course, and a cook to prepare meals—she entertained a good deal and loved to drive around in her expensive foreign imported car, tearing along at speeds that sent Stephanie's heart into her mouth if she and the children were also in the car. Matt would grip the seat, white to his hairline. Elnora would turn green and whisper to her, 'Stevie, I feel sick.' Viola Burgess sometimes laughed and slowed down or parked to let her little girl walk off the sickness. Sometimes, though, she swore and put her foot down, accelerating, making the car bump and roar until Elnora threw up, and then Viola would turn round and start hitting her hysterically while the child sobbed and shivered. If Stephanie said a word, tried to intervene, Viola would begin screaming at her, calling her names that Stephanie had never been called before, using words she had never heard spoken aloud, only seen written on walls. She was aghast and unable to do anything but back away.

The climax came on the morning after a party at a neighbour's farm. Stephanie had danced with Gerard for hours. She had been in another world. The

memory, the reflection of that intense happiness, was
in her face when Viola walked in on her the following
day and launched her attack.

'I don't want you running after Gerard Tenniel, do
you hear me? He isn't interested in a little schoolgirl
like you. He's sophisticated, a man of the world. You
just embarrass him, I could see he didn't know what to
do last night; he wanted to dance with me, but you
clung round his neck like a limpet. If I see you chasing
him again you'll be fired!'

Stephanie had made the mistake of protesting,
arguing with her. She had been appalled and terrified
by the outpourings she had to listen to after that.
Viola's face was shrill and hysterical. She had lost
control, and Stephanie had suddenly realised that
Viola was furiously jealous of her. Viola fancied
Gerard herself; she was very angry because instead of
pursuing her he had shown so much interest in her
children's nanny.

It was as if the beauty and gloss had been wiped out
from her face abruptly leaving another woman staring
at Stephanie, distorted, violent, dangerous. The
threats grew more and more shrill. 'You're not to see
him again! Gerard comes here to see me, not you.
Leave him alone, do you understand? Leave him
alone. Gerard's mine!'

When Stephanie just stared, aghast, Viola flew into
one of her manic rages and began hitting her. She tried
to get away and was knocked off her feet, sprawling
helplessly on the carpet. Viola kicked her in the ribs
and Stephanie gave a hoarse gasp of pain, but then the
door opened and Theo Burgess ran across the room,
white and horrified.

He pushed his wife away from the girl and knelt

down, putting his arm under her to lift her. 'My God, Stevie, are you hurt? What did she do to you? I'm so sorry, my dear, don't cry like that.' He brushed a shaking hand over her tumbled hair, stroking it. 'Don't, my little love. I won't let her near you again.' He kissed her forehead gently while Stephanie froze in shock at the tenderness in his voice. It hadn't occurred to her that Theo had become so fond of her. 'My poor little love, I should never have let her out, she's been getting worse lately, but I hoped . . .'

Stephanie interrupted him, a scream breaking from her throat as over his shoulder she saw Viola, completely mad, face unlike anything Stephanie had imagined in her worst nightmares, with a gun in her hand. It was Theo's gun which he kept locked in a drawer beside his bed in case of intruders in the night. God knew how Viola had got hold of it. She must have forced the lock.

Theo looked round and became rigid, and Viola laughed.

'Oh, yes, you're scared now, aren't you?' She waved the gun at them, laughing in that shrill, crazy way. 'So you're going to put me back in that madhouse—not on your life! I'm not going back there, never, do you hear? I'm not crazy, there's nothing wrong with me, you just want to get rid of me so that you can have her, that sly bitch—what's she got anyway? Gerard's after her, now you. She must be hot in bed to have you both on a string!'

'Viola, you're upset, now listen to me,' Theo said very carefully, beginning to get up.

'I'm sick of listening to you! Goodbye.'

For a second or two, Stephanie didn't believe it had happened. She was kneeling, staring, her ears deafened by the crash of the shots, and Theo was slumping over her and pinioning her body under his. Viola stalked over to them both, the gun still pointing, but now it was aimed at Stephanie's face and her finger was slowly squeezing the trigger while she laughed down at the girl's terrified face.

That was when Stephanie fainted, and woke up to find herself in the centre of a maelstrom.

CHAPTER FOUR

She couldn't hide inside her flat for ever, of course. An hour or so after she got back from the hotel, Robert tapped on her door. 'Are you up yet, Sleeping Beauty?' he called, teasing in his voice. He must have thought she hadn't been awake long, because he looked surprised when she opened her door fully dressed and wearing make-up. At least he hadn't heard her go out and return; he wouldn't guess how much had happened since he last saw her. She seemed to be a million miles from the girl who, only yesterday morning, had set off for work, never suspecting that in a very few hours her life was going to be blown apart for the second time.

'How's the head this morning?' Robert asked, eyeing her. 'You still look pale and you've got shopping bags under your eyes.'

Stephanie managed a smile. 'Oh, thanks, you're such a comfort. That makes me feel just great!'

'Come and have breakfast with us,' he invited. 'I'm a messenger from Gwen; she's making waffles, and there's your favourite maple syrup.'

'Lovely,' she said, following him to the sunlit kitchen, Gwen was in her oldest jeans and a pink tank top, a butcher's apron over her clothes, waiting with a jug of waffle mix for them to arrive. 'Right,' she said, pouring the batter into the hot waffle iron. 'This is Rob's, okay, Stevie? You're next.'

They never had time for enjoying breakfast during

the week. They all grabbed a cup of coffee and a slice of toast and ran. Sundays were a bit of a ritual. Gwen enjoyed cooking when she got the time, and surprised them with a variety of different breakfasts.

This was the last breakfast Stephanie would eat with them. The thought kept chiming in her head; it had a mournful sound. She was glad they didn't know. They were both very cheerful, arguing over who got the funny section from the Sunday paper, talking about planting a new lilac tree in the garden later that year, discussing the front-page headlines with indignation. It was an ordinary Sunday and she didn't want to ruin it even by a hint that anything was wrong.

Would Robert ever forgive her? He had been a wonderful brother: after she came back from Australia he had insisted she live with him, and as soon as he and Gwen bought this house they turned the spare rooms over their garage into a flat for her. She had sometimes wondered if Robert kept such a careful eye on her because he had some reservations about what had really happened five years ago. He'd never said anything, hinted that he doubted her story, but had he secretly wondered if she was suppressing anything? The trouble with mud is that if it hits you, it sticks, and enough mud had been thrown at Stephanie during Viola's trial. Her family had stoutly insisted on her complete innocence; the prosecution had built their case around the accused's long history of intermittent schizophrenia. From their point of view, Stephanie was simply irrelevant. Viola had become dangerously violent from time to time long before Stephanie arrived on the scene. It had been Viola and her defence team who had accused Stephanie of having an affair with Theo Burgess. Viola did not make the mistake of mentioning her jealousy over Gerard—that might have ruined her case. She had concentrated on the lie about Stephanie and Theo and made it so convincing that Stephanie almost came to believe it herself.

On the day when she was giving evidence she had been asked about what Theo had said as he knelt beside her, holding her in his arms. She should have lied; she tried not to answer. She stammered, flushed and unhappy, but in the end she had to admit that Theo had called her 'my little love'.

She could never forget the intake of breath in the court, the way people exchanged looks. Viola's eyes had glowed with triumph; catlike, malicious. Stephanie had betrayed herself, making Viola's case for her.

What could she have done? She had protested that she had no idea why Theo had said it, there had never been anything between them, Theo was just her employer, but there was so much evidence from other sources—of her and Theo playing in the pool with the children, the hours they spent together while Viola was out at parties or driving around in her fast car. When witnesses stressed how unpleasant, how violent, Viola could be, they also admitted that Theo and the children had been much happier after Stephanie arrived. Somehow, it became far more believable that Theo, badgered and unhappy with his wife, had turned to the young girl who was managing to make life easier for him. Stephanie had been convicted without ever being charged, guilty at least of contemplating adultery if not actually committing it.

Viola had been found guilty, but on grounds of diminished responsibility, because of her schizophrenia, she was committed to the mental hospital

within the prison system. The two children were taken
to live with their aunt in Sydney. Stephanie fled for
England, where the case had not made headlines and
nobody recognised her.

She had not been on trial, but she had been found
guilty; conversation buzzed and people stared at her
wherever she went in Queensland. Everyone believed
that she had been Theo's lover; she couldn't even
defend herself because such rumour was a hydra-
headed monster. Nobody actually asked her directly.
She couldn't deny it; she could only flinch under the
curiosity and disapproval.

Gerard had swallowed the story, hook, line and
sinker—his silent contempt in that courtroom had
made Stephanie's ordeal that much more painful, and
when she went back to England she had hoped she
would never see him again.

'So, what are we going to do today?' Robert asked
her and Gwen, throwing down the Sunday paper he
had been reading.

'The washing,' said Gwen, and he made a face.

'Not this morning, Gwen. Can't it wait?'

'Will your shirts wait? Will your underpants? Or is
that an indelicate question?'

'You are putting my little sister off marriage,'
Robert said reprovingly. 'She'll think that's all there is
to it—waffles and underpants.'

'You said it, not me,' retorted Gwen, taking the
dirty plates into the kitchen and dumping then in the
dishwasher. The house was crammed with labour-
saving devices to save them both time, but somebody
had to load the washing machine and hang out the
washing, and it was usually Gwen or Stephanie.
Robert pleaded ignorance of such complicated ma-

chinery; to prove his point he once volunteered to do the wash and managed to turn Gwen's favourite white sweater bright pink by washing it with a pair of his maroon socks. Since then, Gwen hadn't let him near the washing machine, but Stephanie had the strong suspicion that there had been method in her dear brother's madness.

Stephanie got up. 'Euan may be coming round for me later, so why don't I stay here and do the washing and tidy up for you while you and Rob drive out to the country?' she suggested to Gwen, who gave her an uncertain, grateful look.

'Are you sure? It will take an hour or so, you know, Stevie. I can manage it.'

'Help me talk her into it,' Stephanie said to her brother, who laughed.

'Come on, Gwennie, grab your jacket and let's go before baby sister changes her mind. We're not on call, damn it. Let's see the world for a few hours.'

Gwen gave Stephanie a hug. 'You're an angel, thanks. I've put the washing in the basket. Shall I sort it out for you before I go?'

'I can read labels, thanks, and I don't wash maroon socks with people's new white sweaters.'

'Ouch!' said Robert, taking his wife's hand and dragging her away, still talking earnestly about whites and woollens and water temperatures.

When their car had gone Stephanie methodically began to do the washing; it helped to stop her thinking. She did some housework and then sat down to write letters. They were very hard to write. There was so much she wanted to say.

She took several hours over them and when they were in their envelopes she hid them in her handbag.

Euan drove up to the house at three in the afternoon. He was expected to have Sunday lunch at home with his mother; Stephanie never saw him for that meal.

He looked sharply at her as she opened the door. 'Hallo, how are you today?'

'I'm fine.' Her answer was automatic, but his searching stare made her uneasily aware that she didn't look so terrific.

'I think you should have spent the day in bed,' Euan thought aloud in a professional tone. 'It could be the start of 'flu; there's a lot of it going around town.' He looked past her. 'Where are Rob and Gwen.'

'Out. A drive in the country, lunch somewhere special.'

'That's what you need—a country drive,' decided Euan, and whisked her out to his car.

He talked as they drove, but Stephanie found it hard to concentrate on what he was saying and she didn't say much herself. The unexpected spring sunshine had brought out a crowd of other Sunday drivers; the roads were far from empty.

Suddenly Stephanie was alerted by hearing Gerard's name. She looked round at Euan, who was talking lightly.

'Odd chap, though. My mother was surprised to see him; she'd sent an invitation to his mother, but she hadn't expected Tenniel to turn up out of the blue. I suppose he was killing two birds with one stone—had business down here and dropped in on the party while he was in the neighbourhood.' Euan laughed shortly. 'My mother seems to think he's a ladykiller. That's what his mother claims, anyway. I suppose he's a good looking guy. What did you think of him, Stevie?'

She took a deep breath, the truth jamming up her mind. She simply wouldn't know where to start answering that. So she fell back on a dry generalisation.

'I distrust fair men.'

'Tall, dark and handsome for you?' Euan looked round at her, grinning. 'I'm not in the running, then? Why didn't you warn me? Is it too late to have my hair dyed?'

She managed a pretence of a smile. 'I like red hair; it's different.'

'They used to call me Foxy at school. That really got my goat.'

Stephanie felt a heavy sadness, looking at him secretly, realising with a bitter qualm how close they had become to being happy together. If Gerard Tenniel hadn't turned up at the party Euan might have proposed this weekend and she would have said yes, without a second's hesitation. She had been expecting it and there had been no doubt in her mind that she wanted to marry him.

Why had life played such a lousy trick on her a second time? Why did Gerard Tenniel have to be Euan's mother's godson?

They drove for some twenty miles along the coast, watching the sea dance and glitter as if the waves were silver scales on a million leaping fish. By the time they got back to Wyville it was dusk. They had a light supper in a seafood restaurant along the front; the place was crowded, it was a popular eating place. There was no privacy for them, but tonight Stephanie was relieved about that. She did not want to be alone with Euan now.

They had to park at the far end of the sea front, so

they walked slowly back there at about nine, Euan's arm around Stephanie's waist. Just before they reached the car they met Gerard Tenniel who was strolling along the front too, his hands in his pockets and his body lazily graceful.

'Hi, still here?' Euan asked, surprised.

'Yes. I leave tomorrow,' said Gerard, his eyes resting on the way in which Stephanie and Euan were entwined. He looked slowly upward and Stephanie defiantly met his gaze, refusing to be intimidated by the hard glint in those grey eyes. Let him stare. What could he do about it? This was her last time with Euan. The very last time.

'You remember Stephanie?' said Euan politely, oblivious of any tension in the atmosphere.

'Vividly,' Gerard drawled.

'We've just had a marvellous day out—drove right down the coast, came back, had a lobster supper—very indigestible and loaded with calories, but it was delicious, wasn't it, Stevie?'

'Don't you have to get up early tomorrow?' enquired Gerard with a little, malicious smile.

'Don't remind us—yes. Back to the labour camp at crack of dawn. You picked the right profession, Tenniel—all those bar dinners and expense-account lunches! Only a fool chooses to be a doctor.'

'You love it,' Stephanie said angrily, leaning on him. He was a wonderful man; she was going to miss him badly.

Mildly surprised, Euan looked down at her, smiling. 'So I do, darling, thanks for reminding me.' He glanced at his watch. 'We must rush now, Tenniel—nice to see you. Give my respects to your mother.'

'I will,' said Gerard, watching him unlock his car.

Stephanie stood there, waiting to get into the passenger seat, not allowing her eyes to stray towards Gerard, but she felt him watching her, was conscious of the secret reminder in his stare.

Euan opened the door for her and she slid with relief into her seat.

'See you,' said Gerard softly.

'Yes, have a good journey back tomorrow,' said Euan, blithely unaware of the hidden meaning in Gerard's light words.

They drove away, and Stephanie found herself shaking violently. Time was running out. Tomorrow would soon be here. And what was she going to do about Gerard Tenniel and his blackmail?

She left the house next morning at her usual time, but her car boot was packed with her cases and in her handbag she had the letters she had written. She posted them on the way to the hotel. Robert had already left, but Gwen was still on the night shift and would be sleeping late today. Stephanie looked up at the windows of the house, her face melancholy. She had been happy here.

Then she looked away and started the car. There was no point in sitting here brooding; she had learnt that five years ago. You didn't just lie there when fate knocked you off your feet! You made yourself get up, even if it took a long time, even if you had to crawl on your knees at first. It had taken her a long time to get over the murder and then the trial. Depression had been the worst part of the process of recovery; some days she felt as if she saw everything through a black filter. The world was dark for her, her food tasteless, her body lethargic. But she had got over that too, in time, and come through to a sunlit plain here in Wyville, with her job, her friends, her brother and his wife, and Euan.

And Euan. She bit down on her lower lip; she mustn't even think about Euan. It was going to hurt whenever she did, and it was wise to avoid the occasion of pain.

When she got to the hotel, there was no one on reception except the night porter, who was sorting through the day's post and whistling through his two front teeth in a penetrating way.

'Hallo, sunshine,' he said, looking up as she walked towards him. 'Who stole your smile?'

She pretended to laugh. 'I had a tiring weekend.'

'Why don't you marry the guy? He wouldn't keep you up at night then.' The night porter grinned delightedly at her blush.

'Is the boss down yet?' Stephanie asked huskily.

'Still eating his breakfast. Oh! I forgot—there was a message for you from one of the guests.' He consulted the pad beside the telephone. 'Mr Tenniel. He said he'd like to see you the minute you came in.'

Stephanie nodded wearily. 'I'll go up and see him now.'

'Is he a problem?' The porter watched her curiously. 'Want me to deal with it?'

She laughed, her eyes feverish. 'No, thanks, I'll see to it myself.'

Gerard was fully dressed when he opened his door. He gave her a cool nod, his eyes probing her pale face. 'Come in.'

When the door closed he gestured to his two pigskin cases. 'I'm packed and ready to go. I saw the manager last night, paid my bill and told him I was taking you with me.'

Her eyes flew upwards to read his expression. 'What did you say to him?'

'Don't look so tense! I told him I'd offered you a new job in London.'

'What?'

'And I compensated him for the inconvenience of having to find someone to take your place.'

'You had no right . . . you told him I was going away with you?' Stephanie had gone white, her eyes horrified. 'Why on earth did you do that? Can't you see he'll tell my brother? This is a small town; everyone knows everyone else. It will be common gossip inside twenty-fours hours. Robert will know where to find me and he'll come looking for me. My God . . .'

'Did you intend to vanish from your brother's life for ever?'

The dry question stopped her in her tracks, and she stared at him in dumb misery. At last she whispered, 'What else can I do?'

His face reflected impatience, a dry sarcasm. 'What an extremist you are, Stephanie!'

'You dare say that to me?' A rush of rage sent colour surging through her face and her blue eyes flashed. 'You blackmailed me . . .'

He put a hand over her mouth. 'Do you want the world to hear you? I thought you were afraid of people finding out about your past?'

She was angry enough to bite and he snatched his hand away, looking at the two small impressions on his skin with lifted brows.

'I hope you're as passionate in bed as you are out of

it!' He caught her wrist as her hand swung up to hit him. 'No, you don't—not twice, Stephanie. Try that again and you'll wish you hadn't.' He yanked her closer, ignoring her furious struggles. 'Now listen to me—you're a grown woman, an adult, you have a perfect right to live your life your way without consulting your brother. He's not your keeper. If he comes looking for you in London, we'll deal with that without losing our heads.'

'We?' she spat out, infuriated by his calm assumption of rights over her.

His eyes mocked her. 'That's right.' He lifted her hand, his fingers still locked around her wrist. 'We're chained together now,' he murmured, as though that amused him. It did not amuse Stephanie, who pulled helplessly against his strength, trying to free herself, while Gerard watched her useless efforts with dry indulgence.

She gave up at last, breathing thickly. 'You had no right to speak to the manager on my behalf—I've written to him, I said I would.'

'What excuse did you give?'

She looked away, very flushed. 'I didn't. I couldn't bring myself to lie. I just told him I had to leave the job at once, and I was very sorry for the short notice.'

'What did you tell your brother?'

'That's my business.'

'If he does come looking for you, it may well be mine, so you'd better tell me now.'

Irritably she said, 'I told Robert that I'd realised that I could never quite get away from what happened in Australia and I didn't want to cause a lot of gossip and scandal here, so I was going to London, where nobody would even notice me. It's easier to avoid gossip in a big city.'

He nodded, his fingers unlocking from her wrist, and she snatched her hand back, massaging the red mark he had left on her.

'You should have gone before you got involved with Cameron,' he said drily. 'What did you tell *him*?'

She turned away. 'Hadn't you better ring for the porter to take your cases down? We'd better go now before there are too many people about.'

'What did you tell Cameron?'

'That's my affair. Why don't you leave me alone? I'm leaving here, isn't that enough for you?' Her blue eyes burned with bitterness as she stared at him, and Gerard Tenniel considererd her expressionlessly, as if she was a specimen under a microscope.

'Not quite,' he said, then picked up the two pigskin cases. 'We won't bother the porter. Is there a way out of here so that he won't see us leaving together?'

'The back stairs,' she admitted with a sigh, and followed him into the corridor. 'Did you check that you hadn't left anything?'

He paused, frowning. 'Thanks for reminding me— my coat is on a chair over there.'

Stephanie walked over to get it and carried it over her arm as they made their way down the back stairs and out into an alley which led eventually to the car park. She was tense with nerves until they had put his cases into the back of the car and were driving away. At any minute she expected someone to call her name, come running after them, but nobody was about, the car park was empty.

She deliberately took a back route through the town to reach the motorway to London. With any luck they wouldn't pass anyone who might recognise her car or become curious about the man with her. It was still early in the morning and traffic was light on the minor roads. Concentrating on driving did something to ease her ragged nerves; she couldn't spare the energy to think about her own problems and found herself calming down gradually.

As they turned into the motorway and she fed into the faster moving traffic on the three-lane highway she caught the pale silk gleam of Gerard's hair as the wind whipped it sideways.

'Would you rather I drove?' he asked.

'No, I like driving,' Stephanie said, surprised. He hadn't been serious when he said he still wanted her, had he? In the first shock of that conversation yesterday morning she had been too upset to think clearly, but now in the gentle spring light she couldn't believe he had meant it. He had only been trying to frighten her enough to make her leave town. That was why he had come here the minute he had read that letter to his mother from Mrs Cameron. He had been determined to make sure she didn't marry Euan and risk involving the Camerons in an old scandal.

'Can you recommend a good hotel in London?' she asked. 'Not too expensive, I haven't got much money.'

He didn't answer and she looked round at him, searching his cool face with anxious eyes. 'I have to find somewhere to stay until I can get a place of my own,' she stammered.

'You know you'll be living with me.'

The succinct answer made her hands slip on the wheel; the car swerved violently and a vehicle coming up fast on her right only just missed hitting them. The blare of its horn made her jump; it swept past, the driver leaning forward to glare at her, mouthing angry comments on women drivers that she couldn't hear but lip-read without difficulty.

'For God's sake take the next exit off the motorway and pull up as soon as it's safe,' snapped Gerard angrily. 'I'm in no hurry to get killed. From now on, I'll do the driving.'

Stephanie was so disturbed that she obeyed, turning off the motorway and into a quiet country road where she stopped the car and sat there, trembling, her hands on the wheel while she fought for self-control.

'Get out,' Gerard said firmly.

'What did you mean? I'm not living with you,' she muttered.

'This is no place to discuss it. Wait until we get to London. And get out of that driving seat.'

She opened the door and got out, looking angrily at him as he strode round to take her place.

'You can't seriously think that I'd accept that invitation?'

He slid into the driving seat, buckling the seat-belt. 'It wasn't an invitation, it was an order.'

She bent to glare at him through the open window. 'You aren't giving me orders!'

'Get in the car!'

She walked round the other side of the car and got into the passenger seat, so angry she could hardly breathe.

'Do up your seat-belt. Are you hoping to get killed today?'

Her hands fumbled with the belt as she muttered, 'It wouldn't be a bad idea.'

Gerard swivelled in his seat and leaned over to push her hands out of the way, then deftly clipped her belt into place.

'You little coward,' he derided.

She looked up at him, hot and trembling with anger. 'I am not living with you!'

'I'm not letting you out of my sight until we're married,' he drawled, watching the shock of the words hit her as if it gave him great satisfaction.

CHAPTER FIVE

STEPHANIE sat in silence for most of the rest of the journey. Gerard occasionally threw her a brief, amused glance—which she ignored—but he didn't try to talk either. As they came closer to London, the traffic became so heavy that he needed all his attention for the road. Stephanie began to be relieved that he had taken over the wheel. London traffic was nerve-racking; until now she had only driven on the comparatively quiet roads around Wyville. She had a sinking feeling that she wasn't up to the cut-throat standards of city drivers, who wove in and out, used every spare inch of space, or shot out from nowhere forcing their way into the stream of traffic, apparently without turning a hair. She was stiff with tension just watching from the passenger seat, but Gerard seemed completely calm about it all.

The shock of his announcement about getting married had sent her into a frenzy. Her spluttered rage had only made him smile. 'No,' she had kept saying. 'You're crazy! I'd rather die!'

He had started the engine without a word and driven back on to the motorway. Stephanie had kept up a furious monologue for a few minutes until his cool silence had made it impossible for her to carry on, so she lapsed into sullen silence too. When they reached London she would make it crystal clear that here was where they parted. She was neither living with him, sleeping with him nor marrying him. She never wanted to set eyes on him again, in fact. She would drop him off at his house, find a small hotel somewhere not too close to the centre of London, and set about finding a job and somewhere permanent to live.

He hadn't meant it, of course. It was the most insane idea she had heard in her life, and Gerard Tenniel wasn't actually mad, although his idea of what was funny was perverted. That was all his sudden announcement had been—a stupid joke at her expense. Her rage had only amused him, that was why she had shut up in the end. Why let him get any fun out of her helpless fury?

She stared out of the window at the endless vista of roofs and television aerials clustering under a cloudy sky. The lovely spring weather they had been enjoying down in Wyville had avoided London, and she could understand why anyone in their right mind would prefer to stay away from the place.

Gerard shot her a quick look. 'We're here—this is London.'

'I know that,' she said coldly. Did he think she hadn't been here before? The houses were all too small, too close together, too grey. The air was thick with petrol fumes and city dust. There seemed no end to the gloomy streets, blackened yellow bricks and bumper-to-bumper cars. She thought of the cool, clean air she had left behind her, the open miles of sea, the green fields and white cliffs with the gulls skating overhead, and sighed.

'We should be home soon,' he murmured.

She didn't like the way he kept using the plural. 'Where do you live?' she asked, stressing 'you', and Gerard's eyes slid sideways to observe her with dry amusement, but something more—something she liked even less than the way he kept saying 'we'—an unmistakable glint of determination.

'Highgate. Ever heard of it?'

'Vaguely, I think. North London, isn't it?'

He nodded. 'Dick Whittington,' he added, peeling off into a new stream of traffic heading northwards across the city.

Stephanie looked round sharply. 'What?'

'Remember the apprentice boy who became Lord Mayor of London? He heard Bow bells from the top of Highgate Hill.'

'Do you have dreams of becoming Lord Mayor?' she mocked.

'I'm a lawyer, not a merchant.'

That was when a new idea flashed into her head and she sat up, watching him with triumph. There was one aspect he had forgotten.

'Isn't a lawyer just as much at risk from scandal as a doctor?'

Gerard didn't seem worried or taken aback. He drove with calm concentration, smiling.

'It doesn't do him any good to get mixed up in a scandal,' he agreed. 'But as long as he himself isn't involved . . .'

'But, professionally, I must be dynamite for you as much as for Euan!'

'Why?' he asked coolly, turning off the busy main road into a wide, tree-lined avenue which led up a steep hill. 'You were never charged with anything criminal. You were a witness in a murder trial five years ago. So what? If witnesses became immediate social pariahs our courts would be emptied overnight.'

Stephanie stared at him incredulously. They were

moving up the hill on either side of which stood large
Edwardian houses; detached and set among spacious
gardens. She didn't even spare them a glance.

'But ... if it doesn't bother you,' she whispered,
'why did you insist that it would wreck Euan's life?'

Gerard turned the car suddenly and swung into a
wide driveway, pulling up outside one of the Edwardian houses. He switched off the engine and leaned his
arms on the steering wheel, his head swivelled to
regard her almost compassionately.

'I'm not Euan Cameron and I don't have a mother
like his. Do you really think she would let him marry
you once she knew about your adultery with Theo
Burgess?'

'I didn't ...' Stephanie broke out, flushing. 'I told
you ...'

'His wife shot him over it. Can you see yourself
convincing Mrs Cameron that you were innocent?'

She slackened in her seat, admitting to herself that
he was right, damn him. When she didn't say
anything, Gerard leaned over her and she tensed
nervously, her eyes flicking to his face, but all he did
was unfasten her seat-belt. 'Out you get!'

'Will you stop pushing me around?' she flared. He
hadn't acted this way five years ago; he had been
gentle and considerate. Now his high-handed manner
annoyed her intensely.

He shrugged, getting out of his own seat to walk
round the car. Stephanie saw her chance and slid over
into the vacated driving seat, reaching for the ignition
key.

It wasn't there. Gerard leaned in the other window,
the key swinging from his finger. 'Looking for
something?' His smile teased her briefly, then he was

gone, and she sat rigidly, looking at the house. Ivy clambered over the walls and the building was solidly gracious, very suitable for an eminent barrister, no doubt, but it seemed very large.

Suddenly she realised that he had unlocked the car boot and was getting her cases out. She jumped out and ran to snatch up the case he had put on the tarmac of the drive, then threw it back into the boot. Gerard slapped her hand and withdrew the case again.

'You hit me!' she fumed incredulously. 'Who do you think you are? Give me back my car keys, leave my luggage alone!'

He slipped her car keys into his pocket, his smile lazy, picked up both of her cases and started to walk to the front door. She followed, shaky with rage. 'I'm talking to you! Don't you dare ignore me! Give my car keys back. You're not hijacking me. I'm going to a hotel.'

He put the cases down and Stephanie tensed, waiting for him to turn. She was surging with violence, she wanted to hit him even if it meant he would hit her back. It would let some of the tension out of her. But Gerard Tenniel didn't even look at her. He got a keyring out of his pocket and unlocked the front door, lifted the two pigskin cases into a spacious black and white tiled hall and then turned round and came towards Stephanie before she could back away. One minute she was looking at him angrily—the next she found herself over his shoulder in a fireman's lift, her legs kicking helplessly as he carried her into the house.

'Not quite the traditional way of carrying a bride over the threshold, but it will have to do for now,' he said coolly.

'Put me down,' she shrieked.

Gerard walked into an elegant drawing-room. She had five seconds in which to take in the silk brocade of curtains and upholstery, the cool green and white of the décor, and then he dropped her from a great height on to a couch.

She bounced, breathless at the surprise of it, then burst out again. 'I could have hit my head on that table—how dare you throw me around as if I was a doll?'

'You asked me to put you down.' Gerard turned and walked out. Stephanie scrambled up and looked round the room. There was a piano taking up a great deal of room, a polished mahogany grandfather clock, a white and green carpet, and, through the open door, a view of Gerard stacking her cases in the hall next to his own.

She got to him just as he shut the front door and turned. She collided with him at speed and his arms went round her.

'Such flattering eagerness!' he murmured, and she looked up to glare her fury at him, starting another angry protest.

'I am not . . .'

She never got another syllable out. His mouth hit hers with the force of a floodtide sweeping everything before it. Her head was driven backwards, her body bent helplessly, she could hardly stand and clutched at his shoulders for support. Panic began to rise inside her, she tried to struggle, but he was too strong for her. She had to fight, she had to get away, she told herself, writhing in the inexorable grip of his hands.

For the first time in her life she began to understand what sexual drive really was; Gerard had unleashed it on her and she was dazed and unable to control her own response to it. Her eyes wouldn't stay open, her mind had become sluggish, reluctant to operate, as though the physical power Gerard had over her was also operating at another level, subduing her mind as well as her body. Her senses were busy, though, telling her a dozen things at once about what they were experiencing—the feverish insistence of his mouth, the sensual stroke of his hand up and down her spine, and then he had unzipped her dress and his hand was inside, exploring, travelling without hindrance. He pulled her dress down over her shoulders, lifting his head briefly, then began to kiss her neck, the pale skin above her breasts, her breasts themselves.

That was when Stephanie fought her way out of the sensual spell holding her. She dragged herself away from him, moaning. 'No, no! Stop it.'

Gerard straightened, his hands gripping her bare shoulders, and she stared up at him, aware of tumbled hair, a hotly flushed face.

'You look like a woman who's just made love,' he said, his mouth crooked with satisfaction. 'I used to wonder what you would look like if I kissed you like that, but I was always afraid to try.'

Stephanie suddenly felt a real fear. She hadn't been taking him seriously until now, she had thought he was playing games with her, that eventually he would take her to a hotel. It hadn't seemed possible that he could mean what he said, but the ruthless force of that kiss had changed everything. She looked into his grey eyes searchingly. What sort of man was he?

'Why?' she whispered dazedly.

His brows arched. 'Why? Why do I want you? Is that what you mean? That's a naïve question, isn't it, Stephanie?'

She closed her eyes, shuddering. 'Even if I don't want you?'

The hands tightened on her, hurting, and she winced. 'Five years ago, I fell in love with an illusion. Maybe I helped you to make a fool of me, I deceived myself, I wanted you to be some sort of dream, but even if I have to take some of the blame, you still used me, Stephanie.'

'No!' Her eyes opened, she looked urgently at him. 'I didn't, Gerard, please, believe me, I didn't!'

'You and Burgess.' He bit the name out as if he hated the taste of it.

'There was nothing between me and Theo!'

'Do you expect me to believe that?' He laughed harshly, shaking her. 'Listen to yourself! You call him Theo—your employer, old enough to be your father—but you use his first name, and don't tell me everyone did, because I don't remember you calling him Theo in public. You called him Mr Burgess then. The pair of you were very careful not to let anyone guess, but you knew him intimately, didn't you, Stephanie?'

She shook her head wildly. 'He never touched me. Never kissed me, never said a word you couldn't have heard—it was all lies!'

'Then why did she shoot him?'

'She was a schizophrenic—you know that! She was in a manic phase, liable to do anything, and Theo was in her way. She made up that story about him and me because it gave her an excuse for killing him. She thought she might get off if she invented a reason the jury would sympathise with.'

Gerard considered her coolly, with detachment. She was trembling passionately. He released her shoulders and walked away across the room. 'You need a drink.'

Stephanie stared after him, biting her lip. He hadn't listened, he didn't believe her.

'Brandy?' he asked with his back to her.

She didn't answer. She slowly walked over to the brocade-covered couch and sat down. The cool elegance of the drawing-room mocked her. She stared across it fixedly, seeing Viola Burgess as clearly as if she stood there now; her face distorted by jealous rage. If she told Gerard that Viola had been jealous over him, not over her husband, would he believe her? Why should he, when he didn't believe that she hadn't had an affair with Theo Burgess? It was obvious what he would think—that she was inventing Viola's interest in him to back up her protestations of innocence. He had made up his mind about her. Those cynical eyes would watch her with derision if she tried to tell him the whole truth. She hadn't told anyone about Viola's jealous outbursts over Gerard. Perhaps she should have done, but somehow she couldn't bear to repeat the other woman's words. She had felt sorry for Viola; the woman was sick and would pay a heavy price for what she had done. Stephanie hadn't realised then how heavy a price she herself might have to pay.

Gerard came back to her and sat down on the couch beside her, putting a glass of brandy to her lips. 'Drink it.'

She turned her dilated, distressed eyes on him slowly. 'You frighten me,' she whispered. The helpless inadequacy she had felt a few moments ago in the face of his insistent lovemaking had mirrored the way she felt when Viola hit her, screamed at her. Stephanie found violence terrifying, and she was alone here with a man whose emotions seemed to her as unpredictable as Viola's.

'I'm offering you brandy, not hemlock,' he drawled, his brows lifting. 'Why should you be frightened of a glass of brandy?'

'You know I didn't mean that, stop playing games with me!'

He fastened her fingers around the glass. 'Sit there quietly while I take your cases upstairs.'

'I'm not staying here!'

'We'll talk about that over lunch. I'm hungry— aren't you? We could go out or . . .'

'Go out,' she said hurriedly, too eagerly.

He gave her a mocking smile. 'On second thoughts, I think we'll eat here! You must be tired after your long journey. Wouldn't you like to come up to your bedroom and lie down?'

Stephanie threw the brandy at him.

He saw it coming and was quick enough to turn his face, but the spirit splashed his shirt and waistcoat. He straightened, producing a handkerchief and wiping the wet material without saying a word. Stephanie dropped the empty glass and shrank into a corner of the couch.

'Now I'll have to change out of these wet clothes,' he shrugged, his eyes sardonic. 'You'd better come up with me, I don't think I can trust you down here on your own. Who knows what you might get up to?'

Her lower lip bulged mutinously, and she tried to grip the arm of the couch, but Gerard took her by the waist and pulled her to her feet.

'Will you walk or shall I carry you?' he offered politely.

She walked. At the foot of the stairs he picked up several cases and carried them in her wake. Stephanie tried desperately to think of some way of making him see reason. Viola had been mentally unbalanced; surely Gerard couldn't be? His behaviour might be crazy, but he seemed sane enough apart from that.

He opened the door and carried her cases into the room beyond. 'This okay for you?' he asked, and she looked around her with pleasure. The room was furnished in cream and pink; it was very modern.

'It's beautiful. I love the décor of your house—did you get an interior designer to do it?'

'No, my mother was responsible for all that.'

'Your mother . . .' Stephanie wandered over to the windows and looked out into the large back garden; lawns and rose trees and ornamental shrubs, a number of trees just breaking into vivid new leaf. Although this was London, as her eyes rose to take in the immediate neighbourhood of the house she realised how many trees there were around here. All the houses had large gardens.

Staring out, she went on, 'Your mother's responsible for me being here, too. If she hadn't shown you that letter—why did she, anyway? Where is she? Where does she live? What if she comes here and finds me in the house?'

'My mother and father live in Essex, at Maldon.' Gerard began to unbutton his waistcoat and Stephanie looked round at him in tense alarm.

'What are you doing?'

'Getting undressed.' He slid out of his jacket and untied his tie.

Stephanie measured the distance between herself and the door. Could she get out of this room before he could stop her? She grimly recognised the improbability—he was too fast on his feet.

Gerard smiled politely. 'Sorry about this, but I don't

trust you,' he explained, backing while she stared, wondering what he was going to do now. The next second she knew. The door shut, a key turned in the lock. She was alone, but she was a prisoner.

She ran to the door and banged on it with both fists. 'Let me out! Gerard! Do you hear me? Let me out!'

'Of course I hear you,' he said from the other side of the door. 'I'd have to be deaf not to. Stop getting hysterical. The bathroom door is on your right. Go and have a shower, that will make you feel better. When I've showered and changed I'll prepare lunch and we can talk.'

She heard him walk away and stood with her ear to the door, listening as he walked into some other room. He hadn't sounded irrational just now, perhaps he was still playing some elaborate and unfunny joke on her? From time to time she caught an impression of amusement: a gleam in his eye, a twist of his mouth, as if he was secretly laughing at her.

There was a bolt on the door, so she decisively drew it. She hoped he'd heard that. Turning away, she surveyed the room again. The wallpaper was a delicate cream printed with tiny pink roses, faintly Victorian, Laura Ashley style. The bed was covered with a heavy cream cotton and lace spread and a little heap of heart-shaped cushions lay at the top of it. Each cushion had a red silk ribbon carefully threaded through the material from one side to the other. In the centre where the criss-cross met there was a lovers' knot; loops of red ribbon hanging. The whole room had that Victorian feel; lampshades of pleated cream and gold cotton, curtains printed with ears of wheat and pink poppies, a soft, creamy carpet. Stephanie wandered around, touching things, wishing she could forget the reason why she was here, could stop being so tense and uncertain and merely enjoy this pretty room. She seemed to have been on edge for days. For weeks. But it was less than forty-eight hours since Gerard Tenniel had walked back into her life and started her own private earthquake.

She opened the door into the little bathroom and discovered that that had been given a country touch too. Tiles in smooth cream alternated with an occasional tile which carried a pink rose; the fittings were all in pink and the carpet deep and luxurious, but there was a glass trough along one wall which was filled with plants and behind them a mirror. A mirror on the opposite wall threw back that reflection of green leaves, creating a shadowy greenhouse effect.

Stephanie opened the cabinet of the vanity unit and found a wide array of toiletries—bubble baths, bath oils, perfumed talc, soaps. She chose a bubble bath, ran both taps copiously and poured the contents of the glass bottle into the water, swishing with one hand until the foam began to rise. While she watched it, she wondered how many other women had used this little suite of rooms.

They had been furnished with a woman in mind, that was obvious. She had guessed that long before she went into the bathroom, opened the cupboard and saw all those very feminine toiletries. Even if there hadn't been a selection of very expensive French perfume on the shelves she would have known a woman had used these rooms because she simply couldn't imagine Gerard using any of those perfumed bath oils and talcs. He carried around with him a very masculine fragrance, fresh and cool, more pine than musk.

She slowly stripped off and got into the bath, lying

back with closed eyes. She had to relax somehow, take the edge of this terrible tension.

He had changed. Her mouth twisted angrily. Well, in five years who wouldn't? She had changed, too. She had been a wide-eyed adolescent just passing into womanhood when they first met. Gerard had knocked her for six, hadn't he? He had been unlike any other man she had ever met: glamorous, exciting, sophisticated. She had thought of him as a man of the world, and compared to her own gauche self that was just what he was. She tried to remember exactly how she had felt. Her stomach suddenly clenched in excitement and she knew she had felt that way then. She had been in love with him—why pretend she hadn't? Of course she hadn't known what love was really all about then, she hadn't been mature enough to recognise that those wild highs and melancholy lows were the swings and roundabouts of adolscent infatuation and not real love at all. It had been an unreal love, but it had hurt just the same: she had been uncertain and shy with him, frightened by her own emotions, yet in the grip of such a strong attraction that she had been provocative at times, flirting with him, almost inviting him to kiss her. A second later she would be running away, afraid that he might take her up on the invitation.

With hindsight she knew that it had been a typical first love; it should have been for a boy of her own age, someone as inexperienced as herself. She hadn't had a clue how to handle Gerard Tenniel. She hadn't even realised that he was the one controlling their relationship, he did all the handling. He hadn't been lying when he said that he had treated her with great care. Looking back, she realised now how cleverly he had handled the whole situation. She had been totally unaware of the way he manipulated her, never coming too close, never making her panic. She might well have done if he had turned on the heat; she wouldn't have known how to stop him if he tried to make love to her—but he hadn't, had he? When he did kiss her it had been a light, gentle kiss. She had been restless, clinging, wanting more than that—but if he had offered more she would have been scared witless. Obviously he had sensed as much and kept the lid on his own instincts.

A flush began to burn in her face. She sat up, opening her eyes, sending a little wave of scented bubbles upwards as her body shifted in the bath.

Had he been in love with her? Really in love? That would explain the coldness, the glacial contempt she had seen in his face in court. Had she hurt him?

Gerard had never seemed vulnerable; the idea of him getting hurt was hard to accept, but if that was what lay behind his attitude to her now she had to make him see that Viola had been lying, that she herself had never deceived him or meant to hurt him.

If they could only talk about it, stop this in-fighting, these barbed exchanges, the threats and accusations, then . . .

Stephanie climbed out of the bath, refusing to think about what might happen after that.

She took one of the enormous fluffy bathsheets from the airing cupboard behind the bath and wrapped herself in it, staring at her flushed face in the mirrors. The reflection of the plants crowded in around her, making her look like someone in a jungle peering out, and, oddly, that was just how she felt, trapped in heat and darkness and trying to get out.

She was towelling herself when she heard the

bedroom door being unlocked. Gerard tapped as soon as he realised she had bolted it too.

'Lunch is on the table. A cold meal, I'm afraid—just salad and fruit.'

'I'll come down in five minutes,' she said through the bathroom door, holding her towel in place.

Perhaps if she was calm and matter-of-fact with him he would stop playing this nerve-racking game with her?

'Okay, but don't take too long. I'm ravenous!'

When he had gone back downstairs, she searched through her cases to find something to wear which would make her look cool and composed. She had a strong suspicion that for all his angry hostility, Gerard still thought of her as that eighteen-year-old whom he had manipulated for her own good. It was time he realised that she wasn't an uncertain girl any more— she was an adult woman.

She picked out a pair of white dungarees, a blue cotton top and a white gilet. When she had brushed her rich brown hair until it shone, added some pale pink lipstick and a touch of blue eyeshadow, she looked wryly at her reflection in the mirror.

It was one thing to look calm, quite another to feel it. Still, it helped to know that you gave the impression that you were sure of yourself.

She found Gerard in a sunny kitchen at the back of the house looking into the leafy garden. He glanced round as she came towards him, his brows arching as he took in her appearance.

'There you are. I was just going to pour the wine— white, I hope you approve.'

'Not for me, thank you. I don't drink wine in the

middle of the day, it makes me sleepy. I'll just have some water.'

She sat down and watched him fill his own glass. He gestured to the salad bowl.

'Help yourself.' He sat down and took a slice of roast ham, then offered her the platter of cold meats.

'Thank you.' She took a thin slice of meat and a little salad. 'Isn't this house rather large for a bachelor?' she asked politely, as though they were strangers.

'Much too large,' he agreed, picking up his wine glass.

'Why did you buy it, then?'

'I didn't. I inherited it from my uncle George. He was a bachelor and was born in this house. He died here, too.' Gerard looked at her quickly. 'I hope that doesn't upset you.'

'Why should it? I didn't know him, and I suppose most old houses have seen deaths as well as births.'

'My uncle was eccentric. He only left me the house on condition that I was a bachelor at the time of his death and remained unmarried for ten years.'

Stephanie's fork stopped halfway to her mouth. 'Goodness!'

Gerard grinned wickedly at her. 'Uncle George hadn't thought it through very carefully. When he died I was fifteen.'

She laughed. 'Oh. And not married.'

'No, I wasn't that precocious,' he agreed drily.

Stephanie glanced at him through her lashes, her mouth curving in a faint smile. 'And I suppose the ten years is up now?'

Gerard leaned over the table and kissed her nose. 'Thank you. I've never had a nicer compliment.'

A soft colour invaded her face and she looked down.

Before she could think of anything to say next there was a loud ringing at the front door and Gerard frowned.

'Who on earth can that be?' He threw down his table napkin and stood up reluctantly. 'I'll get rid of whoever it is.' He walked away and she stared after him. For a second she had forgotten that they were enemies. His eyes had smiled across the table, she had smiled back, he had given her that light, teasing kiss on the nose—and she hadn't remembered why she was here, what he had done to her, what he planned to do.

She must have a mind like a sieve. How easy it was to forget! And how some things refused to be forgotten, clinging like limpets in the dark sea caverns of the memory. She had never forgotten Gerard Tenniel or anything that happened in Australia five years ago. Those events, those people, had been stamped indelibly on her mind.

Gerard's voice floated back to her from the hall. 'Julia! What on earth are you doing here?'

'Don't just stand there like an idiot, Gerry, take this box from me, can't you see that I'm giving at the knees under the weight of it?'

'Are you alone?'

'Of course I am. You're hardly very observant—or are you seeing double these days? I knew you'd take to drink sooner or later. All lawyers do, it's a professional hazard. Well, get out of my way, why are you just staring at me? I've come for lunch. Don't worry, I'll get it myself.'

The voice had begun to move nearer as it talked; its owner was obviously coming towards the kitchen and Stephanie sat rigidly, wondering what she should do. Sit there? Hide?

'If you're tired, Julia, go and sit down in the drawing-room—I'll bring you a drink and some sandwiches in five minutes.' Gerard sounded distinctly thrown.

'I wouldn't eat any sandwich you made, I shudder to think what it would taste like.' The kitchen door opened and a tall, *soignée* woman came in, only to stop and stare at Stephanie. 'Oh.' She looked round and said drily to Gerard, 'I see you have company. So that's why you hardly looked thrilled to see me!'

Stephanie stood up, flushing. Obviously, this woman was one of his girl-friends—she looked exactly the type Stephanie would have expected him to go around with. Her clothes were expensive and chic, in the latest fashion. She had silvery blonde hair which she wore in a chignon at the back of her head. Her features had a fine-boned distinction which wasn't easy to classify—not beauty but style was what struck you at first glance.

'Julia, this is Stephanie Stuart,' said Gerard, his mouth straight and impatient. 'Stephanie, this is my cousin, Julia.'

Julia looked thoughtfully at her, offering her hand. 'How do you do? So *you're* Stephanie?'

Gerard and Stephanie exchanged looks; their faces reflected an equal surprise, and Julia looked from one to the other of them, mocking amusement in her face.

'There's no point in beating about the bush—you're why I'm here.'

'What are you talking about?' Gerard demanded.

Julia sauntered over to sit down at the table. 'That salad looks good. Pour me a glass of Chablis, darling, while I fill my plate.' She picked up the salad servers and began heaping lettuce, cucumber, avocado and cress on to a clean plate.

Gerard picked up the bottle of wine and leaned over her, his face dark with rage. 'Don't be so bloody cryptic, Julia. What do you mean—Stephanie's why you're here?'

She picked up the small jug of mayonnaise. 'Is this fresh or from a jar?'

'From a jar,' snapped Gerard, so she put the jug down, wrinkling her nose.

'Lazy swine. You really ought to make it yourself; it tastes so much better.'

'Julia, my patience is wearing thin. Stop dragging this out.' He filled a glass with white wine and handed it to her. 'Why are you here?'

Julia looked mischievously at him, then at Stephanie. 'I had a phone call from your mother an hour ago. It appears that she'd just had an agitated phone call from someone called Robert Stuart.'

'Oh!' Stephanie broke out, her hand flying to her cheek.

Julia watched her, smiling. 'Your brother, I gather.'

Stephanie looked helplessly at Gerard, who asked his cousin, 'What did he want with Mother?'

'Your address, Gerry, dear.' Julia laughed at his expression. 'Your mother rang here, but there was no reply so she got in touch with me to ask if I knew if you were back yet. She was worried, Robert Stuart had breathed fire and brimstone on the phone and Aunt Louise had visions of him shooting you. It seems he said you'd taken his sister away with you. He made it sound positively immoral! What have you been up to, Gerry?'

CHAPTER SIX

STEPHANIE got to her feet, her face distraught. 'I must go—I can't stay here. What if Robert comes to London, tries to find me? He can't find me here, in your house!'

Gerard caught hold of her arm as she ran towards the door. 'Stop panicking. You've got to see him sooner or later, you said so yourself. He has no rights over you. If he does come, you can explain why you left and he'll have to accept your decision.'

She looked bitterly at him. 'I don't seem to be very good at explanations. You never believe a word I say. Why should Robert?'

'He's your brother and, in this case, you're telling the truth.'

'I've never lied to you!'

'Haven't you?' His mouth twisted.

Julia sat listening, her face intrigued and fascinated, calmly eating her lunch all the time as though she was watching television. Stephanie shot her a look, bit her lip. This wasn't the time and place for another of their angry exchanges, not in front of an audience.

'I don't want another argument with you!' she told Gerard, who seemed unimpressed by the assurance.

'Good, then just stop arguing.'

'Oh, why are you so maddening?' she wailed.

'He always is,' Julia intervened.

Gerard turned cold eyes on his cousin. 'Kindly refrain from interfering, we can do without your comments. I don't remember inviting you to lunch, but as you seem to have eaten most of the food now, would you mind leaving?'

'Charming,' said Julia, pushing away her plate and leaning back casually in her chair, quite obviously with no intention of leaving such an entertaining scene. 'I go to all the trouble of coming over here to warn you . . .'

'So that you could find out what was going on!' Gerard interrupted. 'You always were a nosy brat.'

Julia smoothed one stray hair, looking down her nose. 'Brat? Bite your tongue!'

'I can't understand how Robert found out so soon,' Stephanie muttered.

Julia looked at her, smiling. 'Oh, I can tell you that! Apparently he rang the hotel where you worked and they told him you'd gone off with Gerard.' Her bright, teasing eyes flickered to her cousin. 'I can see the headlines now—well-known lawyer arrested for kidnapping.'

'Oh, shut up, Julia!' Gerard snapped.

'Barrister,' corrected Stephanie.

'It does sound more distinguished, doesn't it?' Julia agreed.

Stephanie sighed. 'Oh, what bad luck that Robert rang the hotel—I didn't expect him to find out so soon. I wonder why he rang me? He can't possibly have got my letter so quickly. I only posted it at eight o'clock.'

'If it was a local letter,' said Julia, her face interested in the problem, 'it could have been delivered at midday.'

Stephanie made a wry face. 'I suppose that was it—I'd forgotten the second post. Isn't it typical that the one time when you don't want the post office to be super-efficient they take you by surprise?'

'Absolutely typical,' Julia agreed.

Stephanie decided she liked her. She gave her a thoughtful look. 'I suppose you couldn't recommend an inexpensive but respectable hotel where I could get a room for a few days?'

'You aren't leaving!' Gerard said sharply.

'If you need somewhere to stay tonight, I have a spare room in my flat,' Julia suggested.

'No!' said Gerard immediately, scowling.

'It's just a boxroom, but the bed is comfortable,' Julia said, ignoring him.

'Did you hear what I said?' Gerard almost snarled, grabbing Stephanie by the arm. 'You aren't going. Julia, kindly clear off—you're just confusing the issue.'

His threats didn't seem to bother Julia, and her cool smile made Stephanie feel braver.

'What exactly is the issue I'm supposed to be confusing?' Julia enquired, considering them both thoughtfully.

'There isn't one,' said Stephanie, pulling herself free of Gerard's grip. 'And I'd be very grateful if I could stay the night in your spare room.'

Gerard was distinctly grim-faced now. 'Have you forgotten why you came with me in the first place? That still holds, remember.'

A flicker of uncertainty passed through her face. 'You wouldn't do it,' she said huskily.

'What?' Julia asked intrigued.

'I don't bluff at poker,' Gerard said.

'Liar,' said Julia. 'You always cheated at cards.'

'Oh, for heaven's sake, Julia, will you shut up?'

Stephanie looked questioningly at his cousin. 'Julia, is he . . . unscrupulous?'

'As hell,' Julia said, grinning, then saw the way

Stephanie's face fell and frowned. Gerard gave a dry, triumphant smile.

'She isn't going with you, Julia, you know your way out.'

Julia sat down again, crossing her long slim legs. 'I'm staying. I think Stephanie needs a little female support in this male-dominated household.'

Gerard seethed, his mouth tight with fury. After a moment's consideration of them both, he said through his teeth, 'Out of the question, I'm afraid. There isn't a bedroom available.'

'You've got six of them up there! How many other people are staying?'

'Four of the rooms haven't been used for years: the beds are damp, haven't been aired since last summer.'

'A little damp won't hurt me.'

'You haven't any nightclothes with you. Why don't you go home, Julia?'

'You can borrow a nightie from me,' Stephanie offered.

'Thanks, I will,' said Julia, sauntering to the door. 'I'll go up and choose a room now.'

'You can get pneumonia, sleeping in damp beds!' Gerard threw after her, and she turned at the door to give him a sweet smile.

'I'll air the mattress in front of an electric fire if it seems damp.' She walked through the hall and began to go upstairs.

Stephanie moved to follow, but Gerard got between her and the door with a deft movement. He slammed the kitchen door and leant on it with folded arms.

'I don't want Julia here. Persuade her to leave.'

She met his insistent stare, shaking her head.

'Stephanie,' he said in a softer, coaxing voice, and suddenly he was much too close and she felt her breathing impeded. The anger and tension had vanished from his face and she found the intimate gaze of those grey eyes disturbing. He had changed his tack; what was he up to now? She didn't trust him, but she couldn't quite cope with the way he was looking at her, either. It made her feel as light-headed as it had when she was eighteen.

'How are we going to get to know one another if we aren't alone?' he asked, his hand lifting to touch her cheek.

She stiffened under the tactile seduction, deeply aware of the gentle brush of those fingertips over her skin.

'That isn't the object though, is it?' she said huskily. 'You want to . . .' She broke off, biting her lip.

'Want to?' he prompted, a gleam of irony in his face now.

'Sleep with me,' she finished, very flushed and no longer able to meet his eyes.

'Do you know any better way of exploring the opposite sex?'

Stephanie looked up angrily at the mockery in his voice. 'I won't sleep with you!'

'Do you sleep with Cameron?' The question had the speed and sharpness of a stiletto, and she tensed.

'No!'

He caught her chin, his fingers refusing to let her escape. 'Look at me!'

She looked, defiance in her blue eyes. He leaned very close, staring into them as if reading her mind in them.

'Are you in love with him?'

Her eyes flickered, but she didn't answer.

'Are you?' he insisted.

'I don't know,' she admitted on a painful sigh. 'I

didn't have time to find out. Maybe I was, or maybe I would have been. I like him more than anyone else; we get on well. Euan's the sort of man most girls dream of marrying. He's kind and thoughtful and . . .'

'Good husband material,' he finished for her as she paused, and his mouth took on that mocking cynicism again. 'How long had you known him?'

'A couple of years, but we only started dating less than a year ago.' She knew Euan had been watching her before he asked her out.

'Not love at first sight, then?'

'I don't believe in love at first sight.'

Gerard eyed her oddly, and she felt herself flushing deeply. Her voice had a strangely melancholy sound; a muted regret, as though she wished she did believe in love at first sight. She had fallen for Gerard at first sight, of course, but then that had all been illusory, a wildfire which burnt along her veins for a while and then died out, leaving her weary and disillusioned, no longer willing to believe in any sudden, violent emotion.

That was why she had believed in Euan's caution in approaching her. At least she had been sure that he hadn't rushed into it, that he didn't leap before he looked. She could rely on Euan; he was calm and dependable. She had understood that if Euan did propose it would be because he was utterly certain that she was the sort of wife he wanted.

'Have you ever been in love?' Gerard asked softly.

Stephanie froze, looking up helplessly into the dark-pupilled grey eyes. They held some hypnotic attraction for her; she was afraid she might drown in their depths. He wasn't comfortable, like Euan; he was far from predictable or manageable. He was possessed of some inner power she couldn't describe; a dynamic energy she could feel even without touching him. She saw it surging in his eyes and was drawn to it, helplessly fascinated, like a moth fluttering towards the brightness of a flame even though it knows it will burn up, be utterly destroyed.

She must not let that happen to her; she mustn't let him pull her over the edge. She closed her eyes abruptly, shutting out the sight of his face.

'No,' she said, her voice raw. 'No, never.'

She heard him breathing, very close. His fingers slid from her cheek to her throat and she shivered, backing, until they no longer touched her.

'Never, Stephanie?' he asked, a thread of provocation in his voice, and she knew he was thinking about himself, he was hinting that she might have been in love with him once.

She opened her eyes, more in command of herself now. 'I've thought I was once or twice, but it was a mistake.'

Gerard was frowning now and the softness had vanished from his voice. The sunlight gave his blond hair a burnished look and under it his face was harshly male, brooding eyes the colour of wintry skies, his mouth with the tension of steel cord. Stephanie almost relaxed; the danger had passed, she could resist his male allure when he frowned like that. It was his smile, his sensual gaze, that weakened her knees and made her heart beat far too fast.

'I wish I knew what to make of you,' he muttered, straightening. 'You're as elusive as a cat in the dark. Every time I think I can see you and I reach out for you, you slip though my fingers.'

They both heard Julia's footsteps on the stairs; she was returning. Gerard walked towards the table and began to clear it. Stephanie was still trembling slightly, her nerves jangling from the last few minutes, but she went over to help him.

The door opened and Julia came in smiling. 'The rooms are perfectly aired,' she accused her cousin. 'I've picked one of the big back rooms, next to yours, Stephanie. If you have any nightmares during the night, you can yell for me.' She grinned and Stephanie smiled faintly.

'I will.'

'Or any intruders, of course,' murmured Julia, her eyes on Gerard.

He bared his teeth at her in a pretence of a smile. 'You think you're so funny!'

'How long are you staying in London, Stephanie?' asked Julia, taking no notice of his snarl.

'I was thinking of finding a job here.'

'What sort of job?'

'I've already offered you one,' Gerard snapped.

Julia regarded him curiously. 'In your chambers?'

He nodded. 'As receptionist—ours is leaving. Stephanie can start right away. She'll have to work with the present girl to learn the job.'

'What do you do, Julia?' Stephanie asked as she finished wiping the top of the table.

'Nothing,' Gerard said sarcastically.

'I'm in market research,' Julia said, giving him a pointed look. 'Gerard makes fun of my job but in fact I work very hard.'

'When you work!' he commented.

'All right, the hours are erratic and some days I haven't much to do, but when I'm involved in a project I work all the hours there are.' She went over to a cabinet. 'I feel like some coffee. Want some, Stephanie?'

'Make yourself at home by all means,' grunted

Gerard, going out and slamming the door behind him.

Julia turned, a bag of unground coffee-beans in her hand. 'Dear, dear, aren't we in a temper? Nothing quite as violent as the frustrated male, is there?' She produced a coffee-grinder and began to feed the beans into it.

Shyly, Stephanie said, 'It's very good of you to go to all this trouble for me. I'm very glad of the company.'

Julia finished grinding and emptied the coffee into the top of the percolator. 'Am I allowed to know what's going on? Or is it deadly secret?'

Stephanie hesitated; she didn't feel much like telling someone about her past.

Julia was just pushing the plug into the electric socket and switching on the percolator. 'Don't tell me if you'd rather not,' she murmured without looking round. 'As Gerard always says, I was born nosy. If you want to talk, I can be as discreet as you like, that's all.'

'Are you very close to Gerard?' Stephanie asked curiously. He had never mentioned his cousin to her, but then five years ago they had not done much talking about anything but themselves.

Julia looked round, face wry. 'Almost brother and sister, I suppose. My mother is his mother's twin and they're very close. Well, they're identical, actually, which probably explains why Gerard and I are so alike to look at. He's much older than me, of course.' She grinned. 'I hope you realise that.'

'It did occur to me,' said Stephanie with amusement.

'Ten years, actually. When I was born, he was a horrible knobbly-kneed schoolboy. He claims he used to push me in my pram. I know he used to swing me when I was a toddler, I remember that! My mother watched him like a hawk, afraid he'd push too hard and kill her precious infant. I'm an only child. A late thought on the part of my parents—my mother was thirty-two when I was born, and she claims she hated giving birth so much that she didn't want any more babies.'

'I have a sister and a brother, both older than me. I was an afterthought, too.'

The doorbell rang violently and Stephanie tensed, going pale. 'Robert!' she whispered, staring at Julia.

'It can't be, surely? I'm sure Aunt Louise said that he was coming from the West Country somewhere. He couldn't get here that fast.' Julia looked at her watch, then looked taken aback 'Good heavens, I've been here nearly two hours now, so if he rang Aunt Louise an hour before she rang me ...' She looked at Stephanie uneasily.

'It is him,' Stephanie said, moistening her lips. She didn't think she could face Robert at this moment. What on earth was she to say to him?

'We don't have to answer the door,' Julia suggested, but as she was speaking they both heard movements in the hall, then Gerard opening the front door. 'Too late,' said Julia, looking closely at Stephanie. 'I wish I knew what was going on ...'

'You bastard!' Robert's angry voice made them both jump. It was followed immediately by a crash and Stephanie gasped in horror. What was happening out there?

'That sounded like china,' Julia deduced. 'I bet it was that jardinière that Gerard payed a hundred pounds for last year.'

The front door slammed, but from the raised voices it was obvious that Robert was inside the house now. Gerard was talking curtly, but they couldn't hear what he said because Robert kept shouting over his voice.

'Do you want the police called in on this,' he bellowed, and a moment later, 'Don't lie to me! My sister wouldn't just vanish without a word to me unless something was wrong.'

Stephanie went shakily to the kitchen door and opened it. She had no option; she couldn't cower in here while Robert broke up Gerard's home. The hall was littered with earth and broken china.

Her brother was facing her; his eyes flashed past Gerard and fixed on her. 'Stephanie! Are you all right?'

Gerard glanced back over his shoulder; she got the feeling that he had been holding her brother at bay, making sure that he did not get past him and reach the kitchen.

'I'm okay, Robert,' she said flatly, and walked towards him with Julia in the doorway behind her, watching intently. Stephanie caught a look of relief in Robert's face as he noticed Julia, and flushed, guessing what that expression meant. He was glad to see another woman in the house. She could imagine what he had been suspecting as he drove at some dangerous speed to reach London as fast as possible.

'We'd better go in here,' said Gerard, walking into the drawing-room.

Robert looked at him with dislike. 'I want to talk to my sister alone.'

Stephanie gave Gerard a pleading look. 'Please, leave me with my brother for a few minutes, would you?'

Gerard visibly hesitated, his jaw rigid, then shrugged and went out again. Robert stood in the elegant, tranquil room and stared at his sister as if he had never seen her before.

'What the hell is going on, Stephanie?'

She took a deep breath, wondering where to start. 'Can we sit down, Robert?' Her legs felt so strangely weak, she was afraid that if she didn't sit down she might faint.

He looked around as if only just realising where they were and then threw himself into a chair. Stephanie sat down too, her hands clasped in her lap to stop them shaking.

'Well?' Robert demanded.

'Did you get my letter?'

'Letter? No, what letter?'

'I sent you one, I posted it this morning on . . . on my way. Why did you ring the hotel if you hadn't had my letter?'

'Euan asked me to let you know that he was going away for a few days—he's been asked to go to Saudi to perform a heart operation on a sheikh. They couldn't fly the man over here and they claim they've got all the facilities Euan will need. The Director of their hospital was at medical school with old Bougham, our administrator, and . . . well, it was a typical old-school-tie deal. Euan was told to pack and leave at once, and he couldn't get hold of you at the hotel when he tried to ring. They said you weren't there and there was no answer at home, so he asked me to tell you he wouldn't be keeping his date with you.' Robert's eyes were blistering. 'The date you apparently had no intention of keeping, anyway.'

Stephanie bent her head, very pale. 'I wrote to him . . .'

'Oh, he got one of your letters too, did he?' Robert was scaldingly sarcastic. 'That will be something for him to look forward to reading when he gets back, won't it?'

She kept her eyes down, tears brushing her lashes.

'Robert, don't. I'm sorry . . .'

'Sorry? You vanish, without a word, with a man neither of us ever met before Saturday night and then say you're *sorry*?' Robert's breathing seemed very loud in the quiet room. 'I suppose I can make a good guess at why you went with that bastard—my God, he's a fast worker, I have to say that for him. You hardly saw him for two minutes, but he managed to talk you into going away with him.' He caught her restless movement and watched her in grim silence for a moment. 'Don't tell me you're in love with him—you can't be, not that fast, it isn't humanly possible.'

'I've met him before,' she whispered.

Robert bent forward. 'What?'

She repeated her words and Robert took a deep, audible breath. 'You've met him before? You didn't say so. Where? When?'

'Five years ago.'

Robert stiffened, staring. 'Five years. Did you say five. In Australia?'

Stephanie nodded, her hands tightly gripping, and Robert got out of his chair and came over to sit on the arm of hers, his hand gently cupping her head, turning her face up to him.

'What is this, Stephanie?'

The tears spilled then, and she turned her face into his arm and wept while Robert muttered uneasily and patted her heaving shoulders.

'It's okay, Stevie, don't cry. Come on, there's a good girl, just tell me what's going on. Oh, come on, Stevie—oh, hell!'

She buried her head against him, no longer crying but not wishing to see his face while she told him. She didn't start telling him for a minute because she couldn't find the right words, but Robert was shrewd.

Now that he knew that Gerard Tenniel had somehow known her in Australia five years ago, he began to put two and two together.

'Is that bastard blackmailing you?'

She sat up again, startled, turning a wide-eyed face up to him.

He scowled ferociously. 'So he is!'

'How did you guess?'

'Do you think I'm stupid?'

She laughed, her mouth trembling. 'No, Rob, I wouldn't say you were that. Of course, it isn't blackmail exactly—I mean, we aren't talking about money here.'

Robert still looked grim. 'What are we talking about? What is he blackmailing you for?'

She looked down, flushing.

'My God, I'll kill him,' gritted Robert. He sounded as if he couldn't breathe properly. 'The man's a lawyer, a barrister, for heaven's sake. And he actually blackmailed you into going away with him, moving in here with him.' He stopped abruptly and looked at her, embarrassed, uneasy. 'Stevie, you haven't . . .'

She looked blankly at him. 'Haven't what?'

Robert made a confused gesture with his hand. 'Well, you know.' He was pointing upward and Stephanie's bewildered gaze went up to the ceiling.

Then she caught on and turned a scalding crimson. 'No, I haven't! Robert! You don't think I'd let him talk me into bed—you didn't really think I'd be that stupid?'

'You let him talk you into coming away with him.'

'That was different. In a way, he was right.'

'Right? For God's sake, what the hell do you mean, right? Right to blackmail you?'

'Of course not, that's irrelevant in a way.'

'What is? The blackmail? Irrelevant to what? Stephanie, sometimes I don't think you're quite right in the head. This guy comes out of the blue and starts blackmailing you about something that happened years ago and you say it's irrelevant?'

'Look, just for a minute, leave the blackmail out of it . . .'

'How can I do that? The blackmail's the whole thing, that's what we're talking about!'

'No,' she said, getting up because she knew she would only make him listen and understand if he stopped thinking about her as his helpless little sister who had to be protected for her own good. Robert had something in common with Gerard Tenniel, although he wouldn't be too happy if she told him as much. So she stood there facing him, head up, chin defiant. 'Listen, Robert, just listen and let me explain, stop interrupting and shouting at me.'

Robert looked offended and furious. 'Shouting? Me? I'm not shouting at you! When have you ever heard me raise my voice to you?'

She turned and walked away across the drawing-room to the high bay windows, standing there staring out into the tree-lined avenue. The afternoon was wearing into dusk; blue shadows moved under the trees and birds gave poignant last-minute calls.

'Gerard made me realise something I suppose I hadn't wanted to admit—that I couldn't possibly marry Euan and risk the chance that one day someone else might come along and recognise me and resurrect the scandal about the Burgess murder trial. If Euan wasn't a doctor, if his family weren't the way they are, I could tell him the truth and it might not matter, but honestly, Rob, what do you think Mrs Cameron would say if she found out? It isn't just the murder, I wasn't to blame for that—but everyone believed I was Theo Burgess's mistress.'

'I didn't,' Robert said fiercely. 'Mum and Dad didn't.'

Stephanie turned, her smile quivering. 'Thank you. But even if I swore to Mrs Cameron that I was totally innocent, do you think she'd want to have me as a daughter-in-law?'

Robert stared back at her, his jaw clenched. She read in his face the realisation that she was right, but his equal determination not to admit as much, and smiled wearily.

'That's why I went away with Gerard. I wanted to go right away, make a quick break. It seemed simpler than staying, explaining, talking about it. I didn't want to go, I was happy with you and Gwen, I liked my job and living in the town, it's a nice place, but you know how people gossip—if it once got round that I'd been mixed up in something unsavoury I'd never live it down. I'd hate being stared at, whispered about.'

'Why should you be? Even if you were right and any idea of marrying Euan wasn't on, there's no reason to move away. You don't have to tell anybody anything.'

'What if they found out anyway? Gerard Tenniel isn't the only person in the world who knows. It might be a year, two years, even another five, before someone else popped up who knew—but sooner or later it might happen.' She paused, looking at him gently. She loved Robert and she didn't want to hurt him, but she had to point out the obvious, since he hadn't yet seen it. 'And that might be very unfortunate for you, Rob. The hospital board aren't exactly broad-minded, are they? If you were involved in a scandal of that sort, even as my brother, they wouldn't like it, would they?'

She saw his face stiffen, his colour ebb. He stared back at her for a long time without saying anything.

'That's why I can't stay. I don't want to do anything to make life difficult for you and Gwen. You're happy in Wyville, but from now on I wouldn't be because I'd always be looking over my shoulder, waiting for someone else to turn up, for everything to blow up in my face, in our faces, Rob, because you would get just as hurt as I would.'

He swallowed, shifting on the edge of the chair arm. 'We could move, find somewhere . . .'

'And go through the whole process again? Don't you see, Rob, it wouldn't work? You and Gwen would hate to live in a big city, but that's the only place where you can be safe from this sort of gossip because with so many other people around there simply isn't the same curiosity. In a town like Wyville people love to talk about each other and they're at least ten years behind London in their attitudes. I love the town, you know I do, but I know those people. They'd be shocked, they would never feel the same about me again, and I'd hate that.'

Robert got up and came over to her, put his arm around her shoulders, patting her in that helpless way because he didn't quite know how to express how he felt.

'So what are you going to do?'

'Stay in London . . .'

He frowned, his eyes angry. 'Here? With Tenniel?'

Stephanie gave a wry smile, shaking her head. 'No, of course not—I'm only staying here tonight and—don't look like that!—his cousin Julia is staying here too and has already told me that she'll be in the next bedroom and if I need her I only have to shout.' She smiled at him. 'I like her—she's offered to let me use her spare room until I find somewhere of my own. I'll probably move on tomorrow morning.'

'But Tenniel did try to blackmail you? I could call the police and . . .'

'And create an even bigger scandal?'

Robert seethed, frustration in his eyes. 'Why should he get away with such low-down, despicable . . .'

'You broke his jardinière, you'll have to comfort yourself with that,' she said, laughing without real amusement.

'I wish I'd broken him,' Robert burst out, face red. He moved towards the door, as if bent on doing just that, and Stephanie went after him in alarm.

'No, Rob, don't!'

He was in the hall where they found Gerard lurking. Robert charged like a mad bull, his fist swinging. He had been a boxing champion at medical school and his fist connected before Gerard could get out of the way. Gerard went down in a thrashing sprawl, hitting his head on the bottom step of the stairs. Robert stood over him, fists clenched.

'Lay one finger on my sister and you'll have me to deal with, you bastard!' he growled, then swung round to look at Stephanie. 'Keep in touch, let me know where you are and what you're doing.'

'Yes,' she promised, watching Gerard with anxiety. He wasn't moving—had Robert really injured him? Julia came through the kitchen door, staring at her cousin's prone figure with dismay.

'Write!' Robert said. 'You'll write at least once a week, won't you?' He looked at his watch, his face hesitant, uneasy. 'I have to get back. I had a hell of a time getting someone to stand in for me and I swore I'd be there tonight. I swapped rotas with someone and I must get back to fill in for him.'

Julia had knelt down beside Gerard. 'Is he dead?' she asked, but although she looked faintly worried her tone wasn't serious.

'I wish he was,' said Robert over his shoulder on his way to the front door. 'When he comes to, tell him that I meant what I said—tell him to keep his hands off my sister!'

Stephanie followed him and Robert turned to kiss her cheek. 'I'm sorry,' she said huskily. 'Very sorry about all this. Give Gwen my love.'

'And Euan?' Robert asked brusquely. 'What am I to tell Euan?'

She looked away, sighing, shrugging. 'He'll get over me.' She looked back at her brother and saw that his eyes were angry.

'Poor Euan,' was all he said, though, and then he was gone and she slowly closed the door.

Gerard sat up, rubbing his jaw. 'Your brother has a fist like a steam-hammer!' He tentatively got to his feet. 'I hope that made him feel better. I thought I'd better let him win that round or he might have stayed all day.'

'He knocked you out cold!' Stephanie spat at him with venom.

He smiled, and she eyed him with doubt. Had he been faking the unconscious stillness? He was probably right; Robert had felt better after hitting him, but if Gerard had been acting, she would have to change her view of him. He was even more deceptive than she had suspected, but then he was a barrister, wasn't he? And she had heard that that profession demanded a considerable acting flair as well as a natural eloquence. She should have remembered that. This man was far from simple, far from easy to understand.

'He had a damned good try,' Gerard agreed coolly. 'I felt a certain sympathy, he was under stress.'

Stephanie stared, dumbfounded. 'Under stress? That must be the biggest understatement of the year!'

He grinned. 'Okay, he was beside himself with rage, is that more accurate? I'm no medic but I decided it would make him less likely to have a brainstorm if I let him hit me and didn't fight back.'

Julia looked amused. 'That's your story, and you're sticking to it, I suppose?'

Gerard grimaced, staring at his shattered jardinière with a rueful expression. Robert had managed to break both the graceful china flowerpot and the tall, matching stand. Among the earth and shreds of china lay a few green leaves, a scatter of pink flowers already limp and crushed.

'What a mess,' he said, and Stephanie felt the words were apt and described her whole situation.

'I'll clear it up in a minute,' offered Julia. 'But what about that coffee? I've kept it hot, bubbling on the hob. You look as if you need some, Stephanie. I know I do. All this drama makes life very draining.'

Stephanie began to laugh wildly, almost hysterically. Julia's calm, dry voice made everything suddenly very funny, but it was a joke on the wild side: black farce. All one could say was that laughing was better than crying.

CHAPTER SEVEN

STEPHANIE didn't think she would sleep that night. Leaving aside the succession of shocks which had hit her over the weekend, the breathtaking rush of events carrying her helplessly before them like a straw on a floodtide, she had never found it easy to sleep in a strange room for the first time. Even on holiday, she was usually wakeful on the first night in a hotel bedroom.

She and Julia had cooked the supper; a delicious paella made with frozen shrimps, shredded chicken and some chunks of garlic sausage added towards the end of the cooking time. Julia had found some turmeric in the larder and coloured the rice a delicate yellow; the spice gave the dish a faintly stronger tang, too. While they worked in the kitchen, talking, getting to know one another, Gerard was in his study, a thick brief spread in front of him, catching up on some of the work he had neglected over the past few days, he told Stephanie.

She went into the room several hours after he began work to tell him that the paella was ready. It was dark by then; he had drawn the deep red velvet curtains across the windows and was reading at his desk, a white angle-lamp fixed so that he could concentrate on the closely typed pages.

It was something of a shock to her to see that he was wearing spectacles, horn-rimmed reading glasses which he pushed down on his nose to study her. The grey eyes seemed abstracted, hardly recognising her.

'Hmm? Yes.'

'Supper's ready.'

He pulled off his spectacles and dropped them casually on the desk. The bright lamplight glittered on his blond hair and gave his eyes the sheen of steel.

'Oh, fine.' He ran his fingers over his eyes, as if he was tired. Stephanie saw fine lines around his mouth and upper cheekbones. The lamplight cruelly intensified that weariness; made him look older than usual. He must be in his late thirties by now. Why hadn't he married? It couldn't have been from lack of opportunity: he was far too good-looking and distinctly eligible. He must be well off—this house would be expensive to maintain.

'What is it?' he asked, getting up and stretching. He was wearing a thin white silk shirt which was more or less transparent; she saw the movement of his muscles rippling under it, the faint brown of his skin. 'I'm hungry,' he said, as if surprised.

'It's paella, and I'm not surprised you're hungry— it's half past eight! I hope you won't get indigestion from eating this late.'

Gerard had taken off his tie and opened his shirt collar; she could see the strong line of his throat.

'Paella? Sounds good.' He turned and she quickly looked away to stare round the room. The walls were lined with books on polished mahogany shelves.

'Are these all law books?' she asked to distract him from thinking about the way she had been watching him.

'Some are, most aren't. I keep my reference books in chambers, all but an essential few.' He watched her go over to glance along the shelves. 'If you want something to read in bed take what you like,' he offered.

'Thanks, perhaps I will, later. But Julia's just serving supper, so . . .' She moved to the door and he followed, switching off his desk lamp.

That plunged the room into darkness, she collided with a chair she hadn't noticed and Gerard exclaimed impatiently.

'What have you done now?'

'Nothing,' she said, conscious of him beside her, a disturbing presence in the darkness. His body had a cool scent but there was a hint of musk under that, as though he had been working so intensely that he had perspired. For a second they both stood there, breathing audibly; then, in a rush of alarm, she reached out and groped for the door, pulled it open and almost stumbled out of the room.

Gerard followed, his eyes gleaming with mockery which she pretended not to notice. They ate the paella and drank a little white wine with it, had coffee, and then she and Julia stacked the dishwasher and tidied the kitchen before they went to watch television for an hour while Gerard went back to his study to work on his brief.

'Are you going to take this job Gerard has offered you?' asked Julia casually, and Stephanie shrugged.

'I might look for a job in another hotel.'

'It isn't as easy to find jobs in London as you might think. Unemployment's as tough here as anywhere else.'

Stephanie chewed her lower lip. 'I know, but . . .' She broke off. How could she tell Julia that she didn't trust Gerard and didn't want to work in his chambers?

'You could try it for a month, see how you got on,' Julia added, and Stephanie looked sharply at her.

'Oh, I've no axe to grind,' said Julia, laughing, reading her expression. 'If you hate the idea of working with Gerard, tell him what to do with his job. But you might find the work interesting and it's probably better paid than the job you had in that hotel. I've heard that hotel jobs aren't exactly highly paid.'

'Far from it,' Stephanie agreed, grimacing. 'But . . .'

'But what? You think Gerard might take advantage of having you working for him?' Julia laughed wickedly. 'Go on, I'm sure you can handle him. Don't think I haven't had to cope with sexual hassle from guys I've worked with—it happens all the time. They have such simple minds. They look at my hair and think: blonde girls are a pushover! Then they try it on. It sometimes takes a few hard slaps before they realise they're not on to a good thing, but you can get your message over in the end.'

Stephanie had begun to laugh. Julia's light dismissal of Gerard's menace as a little sexual hassle made her feel a lot less tense. Perhaps she should take that job? She probably wouldn't see much of him, anyway. He would spend most of his time in court, he wouldn't be in the office very much, and it might be rather interesting to learn something about the law.

'The thing I liked best about working in the hotel was meeting lots of different people,' she said. 'I took a secretarial course, I can do shorthand and typing, but I find it dull, just taking letters and filing—being in a hotel reception was more varied.'

'I expect you'll meet quite a few people in Gerard's chambers.' Julia gave her a teasing look. 'Criminals, solicitors' clerks, policemen . . .'

Stephanie's smile froze. She had met enough policemen and solicitors five years ago; she didn't know if she cared to meet any more of them.

'I'm tired,' she said, getting up. 'I think I'll go to bed now.'

Julia stared after her, looking puzzled. Stephanie said, 'Goodnight,' at the door, then added, 'say goodnight to Gerard for me, I won't disturb him while he's working.'

She went into her own room upstairs and found that a strong wind had got up during the evening. As she opened the door the curtains blew wildly about; she had left the window open and the room was full of cold air. Stephanie shut the door and ran over to close the window, too, shivering. It was bitterly cold in here now.

She went into the bathroom to change into her nightdress. Here it was far warmer. She brushed her hair, staring at herself in the mirror. How odd that she looked no different; she felt as if she had changed radically over the past three days. Three days! Was it so short a time since Gerard Tenniel had walked back into her life? Her blue eyes betrayed confused emotions: anger, uncertainty, a cloudy regret. When Euan got back from Saudi Arabia he would find out that she had gone.

He would miss her, she knew that, because she would miss him too. They had been close friends who might have been lovers—if Euan hadn't been the sort of man he was, by now no doubt they would have been, even if they hadn't talked of marriage. Euan was the product of his environment, a man very much in control of his life and himself, a disciplined man, a careful man, whose work was the breath of his being. He was a brilliant cardiologist; he worked precisely, and with a depth of knowledge and experience that would undoubtedly increase as he grew older. His career was more important to him than anything else in his life. He might miss her, but if she hadn't gone, if she had offered him the choice, she was convinced that, however reluctantly, he would eventually have chosen his career rather than her, if it meant wrecking his reputation. Euan was his mother's son; he disapproved of reckless behaviour, he despised immorality.

She turned away impatiently and decided she would think about all that some other time. If she didn't put Euan and all her problems out of her mind, she'd never sleep tonight.

Still brushing her hair, she wandered into the bedroom just as the outer door opened. Stephanie stiffened, changing colour, as she saw Gerard walk in. His gaze flashed across the room towards her, and only then did she remember that her nightdress was almost transparent: a floating blue silk with a deep v-neck trimmed with white lace. In a certain light you could see right through the material to what was beneath it, and Gerard was staring as if he could do that now.

'What do you want?' she stammered, then wished she had chosen another way of putting the question. He was grinning in a way she found distinctly annoying. 'I mean, get out,' she added hastily.

'I brought you some books, as you forgot to come in and get some,' he said, walking over to drop the three volumes on her bedside table. 'I wasn't sure what you'd like, so I picked out a murder story, a biography and a straight novel, but there's a wide selection in my study, if you prefer to pick them yourself.'

She grabbed up a négligé which matched her nightie and quickly slid into it. Gerard watched. Stephanie wished he would look at something else; his gaze made her very nervous. She tied the wide blue silk belt decisively, and felt less vulnerable.

'Thank you.'

Without taking his eyes off her, he kicked the door shut, and Stephanie felt a jagged stab of alarm.

'I asked you to go,' she reminded him icily, stepping behind a chair and gripping the back of it with both hands. If he came a step nearer, she'd pick the chair up and hit him with it!

He sauntered over while she watched, ready to raise the chair, but Gerard had out-thought her. Before she could lift the chair an inch, he sat down on it.

Stephanie's jaw dropped. He leaned backwards, his head tilted so that he could look up at her, eyes glinting, pure provocation.

'You haven't told me your decision yet.'

'What?' She felt as if her mind was suddenly full of fog, she couldn't see straight, let alone think. Her hyponotised gaze wandered over his sleek fair hair, the brush of his gold-tipped lashes on his cheek, the riveting beauty of those hard cheekbones under his smooth skin. Only at the jawline did he betray a need to shave: the faintest roughness around his chin, a pale stubble that caught the light.

'Made up your mind yet?' he enquired.

'About what?' She stared at the warm curve of his mouth; firm, masculine, sexually intriguing, especially when it smiled the way it was doing now. She had a terrifying desire to lean over and kiss it. It was, she thought numbly, a little like emotional vertigo—one step too far and she might plummet to her doom.

His hand suddenly shot sideways, caught hold of her wrist and yanked abruptly. Stephanie gave a squawk of alarm as she lurched forward, but she didn't hit the floor as she had expected. At the last moment Gerard gave a deft twist and she fell into his lap.

'Don't you . . .' she burst out a second before his mouth closed over hers. She didn't want to shut her eyes, but somebody else seemed to be controlling her; it certainly wasn't her intention to let her lids droop, but they obviously had—or else someone had turned out the lights, because it was very dark, a velvety smothering darkness in which her senses rioted. His mouth was doing things to her that were positively immoral, and his hands led a busy life of their own without Stephanie feeling the energy to halt their restless explorations.

'I don't want this,' she mumbled against his coaxing lips, putting a languid hand on his shoulder to push him away.

He lifted his head obediently and looked at her through half-closed lids; the darkness in which she had been lost seemed to be in his eyes now, in those dilated black pupils, which gave back her own reflection, in soft focus, cloudy, shimmering.

'Don't you?' he murmured, mouth twisting.

'Certainly not,' she said, trying to retie her belt. When had he undone that?

'I don't think you know what you want,' he said, pulling the belt undone again.

'Stop that!' protested Stephanie, wishing that she didn't feel so weak and abandoned when his hand found its way to places where it shouldn't be.

She sat up and tried to get to her feet, but Gerard held her waist with both hands, his eyes fixed on the low, revealing neckline of her nightdress.

'Sooner or later, Stephanie,' he murmured, his voice a silky mixture of threat and promise, then leaned over and kissed her at the the deepest angle of the neckline, where her pale breasts rose out of white lace.

'Don't bet on it!' she snapped, angrily wrenching herself away and managing to stand up again. She was several feet away before Gerard knew anything about it.

'Now, please leave my room before I call Julia,' she said crossly, tying her belt for the third time.

He gave a yawn, smothered by his hand. 'I'm tired, anyway,' he said, as though apologising. 'It will have to keep.'

She would have thrown something at him if she had anything easily to hand, preferably something heavy and potentially lethal.

He sauntered back towards her and she backed, opening the door for him to go through.

Gerard paused. 'By the way, you can have the rest of the week off, but I'd like you to start work on Monday next.'

'I haven't decided yet.'

He shrugged. 'Make up your mind quickly. I'll have to fill the job almost at once.' About to go, he paused again. 'Oh, you do have secretarial skills as well?'

'As well as what?' she asked suspiciously, ready to take offence.

His eyes mocked. 'As well as being trained as a receptionist. What did you think I meant?'

Stephanie wouldn't admit what she had thought he meant. Instead, she said coldly that she was a fully trained secretary and could type and write shorthand at a rapid speed.

'Good. In an emergency we might have to call on your secretarial skills,' he said. 'Goodnight, Stephanie.'

She bolted the door behind him loudly and heard him laugh before he went across to his own room. How much of all that had Julia heard? she wondered as she climbed into bed and began to look at the books he had brought her. A fine bodyguard she was! Or was she in bed and asleep already?

Stephanie sat up for a while reading the murder story Gerard had brought her. It was after midnight before she put out her light and long after one before she finally slept.

She woke up in the morning to the smell of coffee and bacon floating up the stairs. Julia called a moment later. 'Want your breakfast in bed?'

Stephanie leapt out of bed and went to open the bedroom door. 'No, thanks, I'll come down in five minutes.'

'Any later than that and the food will have dried to a husk,' Julia told her, going back to the kitchen, and Stephanie flew into the bathroom, washed and dressed at record speed and took the stairs two at a time. It wasn't until she entered the kitchen that she discovered three things: it was raining, it was nearly ten in the morning, and Gerard had already left for work.

'Speedy must be your middle name,' said Julia, going to fish her plate of bacon and mushrooms from the electric hostess trolley. 'Careful, the plate's hot,' she warned, placing it before Stephanie.

'Thanks. It's very good of you to cook this for me. I'm sorry I overslept, but I couldn't get to sleep last night. How long have you been up?'

'Since eight. I'm an insomniac, I only ever get six hours at the maximum. I came down just as Gerard was leaving—he was out of the house by five to eight.'

Julia poured coffee for both of them and sat down, smiling. Stephanie said, 'Julia, you mentioned a spare room in your flat?'

Julia looked at her and nodded. 'If you want it, it's yours.'

'On a strictly business basis,' replied Stephanie

quickly. 'That is, I'd like to pay rent. I don't know if
you meant a purely short term arrangement or
something more permanent?'

'Up to you. I have shared my flat from time to time
and I'm ready to let you have the room short or long-
term, just as you like. We could see how we got on,
couldn't we? We may be incompatible as flatmates. I
once met a very nice Swedish girl when I was running
a market campaign in Harrods. At first sight we hit it
off like mad. She moved into the flat on a Monday and
by the Saturday she'd seduced my boy-friend and
broken my favourite LP. She had to go.'

Stephanie giggled. 'Which did you regret most?'

'Oh, the LP. It wasn't in production any more, I
couldn't get another copy. I had a new boy-friend
within the month.'

'Well, I'll try not to break anything and I promise I
won't seduce your boy-friend.'

'He's not in London at the moment; he flew to Rio
last week and won't be back for three months. He's a
biologist and is out there to study the local flora and
fauna.' Julia smiled. 'And I just hope the local fauna
doesn't include the human variety! I haven't been very
lucky with my men in the past. I never seem to meet
the faithful sort.'

'Who does?' Stephanie said lightly. She might have
thought of Euan, but somehow she didn't, she thought
of Gerard and wondered how faithful he was and how
many other women there had been in his life in the
past five years. He hadn't married any of them, but
that didn't prove anything. He didn't give the
impression of being the type who broods alone over a
broken heart. All that stuff about how he had felt
about her was probably just moonshine, a fairy story
he'd invented because five years ago she had bruised

his male ego. Gerard Tenniel probably wasn't used to
discovering that the woman he had his eye on
apparently had her eye fixed elsewhere.

She must be very careful not to let him know how
seriously she had been attracted to him, how hurt she
had been when he dropped her like a hot brick.

He hadn't been hurt; he'd been insulted. He thought
that she had been using him as a cover for an affair
with an older man, a man he despised, whose only
attraction for her would have had to be money. Gerard
hadn't been jealous of Theo. She didn't believe it. He'd
been personally offended, the blow to his ego all the
more lasting because she hadn't preferred a younger or
more attractive man. She did not accept that he had
had any serious intentions towards her—how could he
have been serious about a naïve eighteen-year-old who
was too inexperienced and shy even to recognise a
sexual invitation when she got it?

If he had genuinely cared for her, he wouldn't have
believed the lies Viola told. He wouldn't have gone
away, vanished from her life. He wouldn't have come
back last weekend and ruthlessly blackmailed her into
coming away with him. He wouldn't have come into
her bedroom last night with the unhidden intention of
seducing her if he could.

He was treating her with mocking cruelty, a
derision she found hard to bear. Only a man driven by
hostility would have come to Wyville determined to
wreck her life, break up any possible chance of
happiness with Euan, force her into flight.

That afternoon, she moved into Julia's flat in
Chelsea. It was small: two bedrooms, a small sitting-
room with a tiny kitchen area at one end of it, and a
bathroom. The décor and furniture were modern and
rather characterless; Julia said she had inherited them

from the previous tenant, and hadn't yet got round to changing anything except to import a few personal items—ornaments, a couple of pictures and some books and records.

Julia wasn't working that week, she admitted cheerfully. Some months she earned considerable sums, other times she had to start budgeting tightly until her next big payment came in. At the moment she was solvent but couldn't afford to be extravagant, so Stephanie's share of the rent would come in handy.

'As I said, I like to check out possible flatmates carefully. You can make some costly mistakes. A friend of mine let someone move in who moved out the same day with half my friend's belongings.'

Stephanie suggested hesitantly, 'Would you like me to get some references?'

Julia laughed. 'Oh, I'm quite good at reading character now. I've met your brother, he seems very respectable—even if he was rather short-tempered.'

Gerard rang that evening and Julia called Stephanie to the phone, her face quizzical. 'Guess who?' she teased, holding out the telephone.

Stephanie flushed and took it reluctantly. 'Hallo?'

'How are you settling in?' asked Gerard, and the sound of his voice had an odd effect on her metabolism. Her body went into overdrive: heart beating too fast, lungs like worn-out bellows, skin icy one minute, feverish the next.

She tried to keep her cool. 'Very well, thank you,' she said in a distant voice.

'Miss me?' he enquired.

Aware of Julia still in the same room, Stephanie kept her remote tone. 'I've been very busy.'

He was quick and shrewd. 'Julia still there?'

'Yes.'

'Can she hear me?'

'Of course not.'

'Good,' he said, a thread of laughter in his voice. 'Why don't you come here for the evening? I'm much more fun than Julia.'

'No, thank you,' she answered with dignity.

'You don't know what you're missing.'

'Yes, I do.'

His voice took on a relentless note. 'Do you, indeed? Who demonstrated?'

Stephanie's face flushed hotly, even though he couldn't see her and Julia couldn't hear him. 'That wasn't what I meant.'

'Are you sure you haven't slept with Cameron?'

'No, I haven't,' she said angrily. 'I've got to go now, goodbye.'

She hung up without waiting for him to say any more, and Julia watched her thoughtfully as she turned away from the phone.

'Gerard's okay, you know,' she said quietly. 'I've known him all my life. He can be maddening, he's as clever as a wagonload of monkeys, he's tough and ambitious and damned good at his job, and he's okay. If I was in trouble I'd bellow for him like a shot. You can trust him, Stephanie.'

'Can I?' Stephanie wasn't so sure. Julia was his cousin, after all. As close as brother and sister, hadn't they said? Of course she would spring to his defence! Gerard was obviously fond of her and had never given her any reason to distrust him. Between Julia and Gerard there was a vital element missing—the sexual conflict which had bedevilled his relationship with Stephanie from the beginning. Once sex enters into any woman's friendship with a man it loads the dice. A friendly game becomes a battle, each determined to

win. With any winner there has to be a loser, and
Stephanie's pride wouldn't let her admit the remotest
possibility of defeat at the hands of Gerard Tenniel.

He wanted to win too much. His ego was involved.
He wasn't fighting fair, he would use any methods,
take any advantage he could, but she wasn't going to
let him beat her.

Julia took her sightseeing next day, from the Tower of
London to Kew Gardens, by bus and by underground
train. They ate their lunch in the cafeteria at the
National Gallery, overlooking Trafalgar Square. The
salad was crisp and delicious, and after the meal they
crossed over into the square to feed the pigeons and
admire the lions and fountains.

Gerard rang again that evening; he sounded far
away. 'I'm in Brighton,' he told her. 'Had to come
down to see a client. The moon's full. My hotel looks
over the sea—you ought to see this moonlight; it
makes the sea seem quite unreal, all silver.'

Stephanie pulled back the curtain at the window
and looked out at the same moon; over London it had
a coppery glow, as though reflecting back the yellow
streetlamps, but it shone on both of them.

'What did you do today?' he asked, and listened
while she told him about Kew and the pigeons and
some buskers she had seen outside a theatre stage
door.

'You won't forget that you start work next Monday?' he prompted. 'Nine o'clock sharp. Julia will give
you the address. I won't see you until then. I've got a
heavy case starting tomorrow and I'll be in court for
the next few days, but with any luck it should be
wrapped up before Monday.'

'What sort of case is it?' she asked curiously.

'Quite simple. A burglary and G.B.H. My client's accused of breaking into a house and hitting the owner over the head with a torch.'

'Is he guilty?'

Gerard's voice was wry. 'My dear girl! You shouldn't ask me questions like that. I told you, I'm defending.' He paused, then asked, 'Heard from home? Your brother? Cameron?'

'No,' she said stiffly. 'I told you, I've been out all day, and anyway, Euan is probably still in Saudi Arabia.'

'If he does show up, you're not to talk to him,' Gerard said brusquely. 'Refer him to me, tell Julia to get rid of him, but don't you see him.'

She didn't even answer that. 'I must go,' she said instead. 'Goodnight, Gerard.'

It was only after she had hung up that it dawned on her that she hadn't said goodbye, her voice had implied that they would talk again soon, and she had called him Gerard, saying his name gently, almost intimately.

She pulled back the curtain again to look at that moon which was shining down on him, too, at the same time. Was he looking up at it, thinking about her?

A shiver ran down her spine. He was sneaking up on her; insidious as spring, inevitable as winter. If she didn't watch out she would find herself in his possession.

CHAPTER EIGHT

STEPHANIE began working in Gerard's chambers the following Monday morning. For some reason, she had imagined that he would work in a prestigious building, a beautifully furnished showplace for the talents of himself and his colleagues. She knew that he was successful and in most other professions success required display, advertisement.

Instead, she found herself going up the steps of an early nineteenth-century house with iron railings at pavement level surrounding the steps down into the basement. The house was in a terrace; it was narrow, three storeys high. The brick was blackened with age and city grime; the stone surrounds of the windows had cracked and become porous; the windows were divided into the original lozenges. It looked like something out of Dickens. Stephanie peered at the brass plate on the wall. Had she come to the wrong address?

'They're all dead,' said a voice behind her, and she jumped, swinging round.

The young man on the step below her grinned. 'Can I help you? I'm a clerk in the firm. Looking for someone?'

'Yes, I'm Stephanie Stuart, and I'm . . .'

'Our new receptionist! Right.' He joined her on the broad top step and pushed open the door into the narrow hall beyond. 'I was told to look out for you. We're upstairs, by the way.' He gestured and she led the way up the very narrow, badly lit stairs. All the way the young man talked to her back.

'I'm Barry Tomkins, junior clerk, I work for the chief clerk, Mr Monday, you'll meet him in a minute. He arrives at nine eleven precisely.'

'Nine eleven?' Stephanie repeated, laughing.

'His train arrives at Kings Cross at five minutes to nine. He walks here, arrives just after ten past.' Barry grinned at her. 'Unless his train is late, which it is about twice a month.' He waved towards a door facing them at the top of the stairs. 'This way, Stephanie. We use first names, by the way, among the secretarial staff, I mean. The barristers are Mr, of course, all except Diana Kenge and she's Miss. Sorry, Ms.'

Stephanie walked into the office and found it empty except for a girl in a neat grey dress who was sitting on a step-ladder filing papers in large black box files. She squinted down at the new arrivals and said, 'Hallo, Barry. You're late!'

'Your watch is wrong again, Lulu.'

'Don't call me Lulu!' she snapped, glaring through her spectacles at him.

'Stephanie, this is Lulu,' said Barry, gesturing upwards. 'She's our senior secretary and thinks she runs the place.'

The dark-haired girl came down the step-ladder with Barry observing her slim legs with interest all the way. She was aware of it and flashed a cool look at him. 'Haven't you got anything to do?'

He saluted smartly. 'Yes, ma'am. Sorry, ma'am. You've got a run in your stockings, ma'am.'

He vanished before she could snap back at him and she turned back to study Stephanie, offering her hand. 'Hallo, I'm Imogen Barber. I'm afraid Joan hasn't arrived yet, but when she does eventually get here she'll explain what your job consists of. She should have typed up a clear description of what has to be done, I've reminded her countless times, but Joan isn't interested in anything but pop music, her boy-friend and having a good time.' Imogen gave Stephanie one of her cool smiles. 'That's why she's leaving.'

'She was fired?'

'Let's say we preferred her to resign. It is essential that clients are efficiently handled, briefs correctly despatched, messages accurately passed on—Joan found that hard. She was more often in the cloakroom than at her desk here; she got telephone messages scrambled, or forgot to pass them on and she lost vital letters.' Imogen consulted her watch. 'And she's late again. She's always late and she always leaves early unless I catch her going out of the door.' Imogen looked at Stephanie hard, as if trying to read her character in her face. 'I hope you're going to do this job rather better than Joan did.'

'I'll do my best.'

Imogen considered her with piercing, remorseless pale blue eyes. 'Then we must hope your best is good enough.'

Charming, thought Stephanie. So this girl worked for Gerard? She looked super-efficient, cold as an iceberg, but very attractive in a streamlined way. No doubt Gerard appreciated the efficiency. Did he find the icy good looks interesting, too?

The door opened and a distinguished man in his late forties walked into the room, nodding to Imogen, giving Stephanie a brief glance.

'Good morning, Mr Beaumont,' said Imogen, and when he had gone through a door on the far side of the cluttered reception area she told Stephanie, 'That was Mr Beaumont, he's our silk, specialises in civil law, very fat fees. The oldest counsel is Mr Allnew; you won't see him for several days, he has a bad cold and Diana's handling his brief for him. She usually dogsbodies for the senior barristers. Mr Allnew is sixty, talks of retiring all the time, but I doubt if he will just yet. He dislikes work, can't stand the law, but he's good. A number of solicitors won't have anyone else. They trust him. He's reliable.'

'Except when he's got a cold?'

Imogen eyed her blankly. 'Is that a joke? I must get back to my own office. My boss will want to dictate some letters.' As she moved away the door opened again and another girl came breathlessly through it, halting as she saw Imogen.

'Late again,' said Imogen, as if more in sorrow than anger. 'What's the point of saying anything to you? This is your replacement, Stephanie Stuart. Try not to teach her any of your bad habits while you train her.'

She vanished, and the new arrival made a furious face at her back. 'Sarcastic cat! She's so perfect she makes me sick.' She pulled off her coat and hung it on a row of pegs behind the door, then smiled at Stephanie. 'Welcome to Colditz. I'm Joan and, thank God, I'm getting out of here, away from Lulu and her sniping.'

'Why do you call her Lulu?'

'Oh, we had an American working here once, she was working her way around the world and spent three months in the office, while one of the other secretaries was off having a baby. She came back afterwards you see, so ... well, anyway, this Yank hated Imogen. It was mutual, Imogen was always getting at her, and the day she left this girl said to Imogen. "You know, you're really a Lulu, you're out of your skull. No job's that important. One day the little men in white coats will come for you, Lulu."' Joan

laughed gleefully. 'Imogen hated it! She went bright
red. And we call her Lulu whenever we want to annoy
her. Me and Barry and Celia, that is—Celia's another
secretary, by the way.'

'The one with the baby? Doesn't she mind leaving it
all day?'

'She hates it, but she hasn't any option—she isn't
married.'

'Oh, I see.'

Joan looked quickly at her. 'She's very sensitive
about it. It was tough on her; Celia's okay. I'd swap
her for a dozen Imogens.'

The door opened and a very tall, thin, black-haired
man came striding in with a frown as his eye fell on
Joan and Stephanie. 'Gossiping again, Joan? I hope
that post is sorted and despatched and the day's
schedule pinned up on the wall?'

Joan gave a weak smile. 'I'm afraid I . . . I've been
explaining the way we do things to Miss Stuart, the
new receptionist, sir.'

The man stared at Stephanie, looked her up and
down, his thin mouth tight. 'I'm the chief clerk, Mr
Monday. I expect my letters to be on my desk when I
arrive. Please remember that.' He looked back at
Joan. 'Get a move on, then!'

After that, the morning was hectic. Stephanie had
little time to notice much beyond the fact that people
came and went at amazing speed; the door was always
opening and shutting. Clients arrived with their
solicitors to see counsel; junior clerks arrived with
briefs under their arm, senior clerks arrived to have a
talk with Mr Monday, uniformed messengers arrived
with parcels and letters, the telephone rang, people
shouted for them. Stephanie was on her feet all the
time and seemed to be awash in a sea of paper. Joan

was helplessly, hopelessly inefficient, that was clear to her immediately. She put things down and forgot where, she got flustered when people shouted, she muddled messages and was obviously bored stiff by the law and everything to do with it.

'What time do you want to go to lunch?' asked Joan at ten to twelve. 'I usually go at one. All the partners vanish then; things quieten down for several hours. They don't see anybody between one and three and often they don't get back from lunch until later than that. Of course, officially, we only get an hour, but the place is peaceful until three and if you're a few minutes late back . . . nobody notices. Except Imogen.'

'Perhaps I ought to go at twelve, if you're going at one? We shouldn't both go at the same time, should we?'

Joan shrugged. 'Please yourself.'

Stephanie left at twelve, intending to familiarise herself with the surrounding neighbourhood as well as snatch a quick light snack. She wasn't hungry; a sandwich or a salad would do.

As she walked away down the street she heard running footsteps and a voice called her name. She looked round to find Barry following her. 'Hi, wait for me. I'll show you the best place around here to eat. Cheapest, too. We all eat there.'

'I'm not very hungry, I was just going to have a sandwich.'

'You'll need more than that to keep you going all afternoon. It's a long day, you may not get away until six.' He put an arm round her to steer her round a corner. 'There's a little café just round here; we call it Luigi's, but the Luigi who ran it died years ago. The new guy answers to the same name, though.' Barry's eyes twinkled. 'You'll love his food.'

Stephanie abandoned her plan of exploring the district and resigned herself to lunch with Barry. He was entertaining and told her a great deal about the firm as they ate the set meal of the day—a shepherd's pie made with grated cheese on the top and served with two vegetables, carrots and brussels sprouts. It was a very cheap meal and Stephanie had to admit the food was good.

Barry was discontented when she insisted on returning to the office by one o'clock. 'Nobody minds if we take a little longer for lunch,' he protested.

'I only started today, I don't want to make a bad impression.'

He slid his arm around her waist as they approached the narrow terraced building. 'You've made a terrific impression on me!'

A car which was pulling away from the kerb slowed; a cold face observed them. Startled, Stephanie looked back into Gerard's narrowed eyes and flushed. Barry suddenly saw Gerard, too, and his hand dropped from her waist. The black limousine purred away and Barry grimaced at her.

'That was our Mr Tenniel, the devil incarnate when he's in one of his moods. I reckon him and Imogen are a couple of bookends; both of them have tongues like scorpions. It's wisest not to fall foul of either of them, but he's the most dangerous. I tease Imogen, but I wouldn't advise teasing Mr Tenniel.'

'I've no intention of teasing him,' Stephanie said coldly, going back to work.

The office was cool and quiet now. The windows were open; spring air circulated, sunshine showed her the small specks of dust floating in the air. Joan had gone to lunch and didn't hurry back. Stephanie cleared the desk and set about investigating the rows of box files on the shelves. She was still confused about her duties. Joan had been working there for months, but she seemed even more confused than Stephanie.

Joan got back at half past two and at around three the flow of people had begun to step up again. There was no sign of either Mr Beaumont or Gerard, but towards the end of the afternoon Diana Kenge came back from court, still wearing her black gown, a parcel of papers under her arm. She took no notice of Stephanie, gave Joan a brief, impatient nod and strode past. She had very short, pale hair and a faintly spotty complexion. She didn't wear make-up and had a myopic look, as well as a faintly worried, hunted expression. Stephanie already knew that Diana was the youngest member of the chambers, a harassed junior doing all the jobs none of the seniors wanted to do, the legal-aid jobs, the poorly paid jobs, the dull cases with neither cash nor kudos to appeal to the experienced barristers.

'Diana's all right, but a bit ratty when she's pushed,' Joan told her. 'I like her better than any of the others.'

'She looked tired.'

'Probably is—they work her to death. Oh, I'll be glad to get out of here!' Joan looked at her watch. 'Quarter to five.' She threw Stephanie a cunning look. 'If I left now I could get the early train and I might get a seat, if I miss that and get the next one I have to stand all the way to St Albans.'

'Is that where you live? It's a long way to come every day.'

'Don't I know it! I'm dead by the time I get home.' Joan gave her another hopeful smile. 'Would you mind if . . .?'

'No, I can manage,' Stephanie said drily. 'Off you go.'

'You're an angel!' smiled Joan, grabbing her coat and handbag and making for the door. 'See you tomorrow—worse luck!'

The door banged and the windows rattled. Imogen came out to see what all the noise was and stared at Stephanie accusingly.

'Where's Joan?' Her eye moved to the peg on which Joan's coat had hung. 'Oh, I see, gone early again. You shouldn't have let her, she knows perfectly well that she shouldn't leave before five-thirty and she was late this morning, so she ought to have worked late.'

Stephanie got up and walked over to the step-ladder to begin filing some case papers which Mr Beaumont had borrowed and wanted put back in their correct box.

Imogen stared up at her, frowning. 'I hope you understand that you can't leave before five-thirty.'

'I understand,' said Stephanie, looking at the dust on her hands. 'Does anybody clean this place? I get filthy just filing a letter. All these boxes are coated in years of dust!'

'That isn't our job. The cleaners come in after we've gone. And they aren't allowed to touch anything.'

'Or clean anything, apparently.' Stephanie climbed down. 'I must go and wash my hands again for about the twentieth time today. It's like working in a coalmine!'

Imogen looked faintly human. 'You could try leaving the cleaners a note asking them to do some dusting, but I'm not sure they'd take any notice. They're a law unto themselves.'

She left half an hour later, looking surprised to find Stephanie still working. 'You can leave at five-thirty,' she pointed out.

'I'll just finish filing these. The tray was crammed

with them and it makes the desk so untidy.'

'See you tomorrow,' said Imogen, smiling.

Stephanie had been working hard since she got back from lunch just to clear the long, wide desk of unnecessary debris. Joan's method of filing was to push everything into an enormous, metal wire tray. Stephanie felt she could almost judge how long some of the documents had been in the tray by the depth of dust between the layers. She couldn't work in a clutter. It made her feel confused, hampered, but although she had been working at full stretch, almost running on tiptoe all day, she already felt she was going to like this job. It was so interesting and varied, so lively. She wasn't sure how much she liked Imogen, but the other people she had met seemed pleasant, and something was happening all the time. She had lost count of the number of people she had met today.

She leaned back in her chair, massaging her back with a groan. Six o'clock. She must go before she noticed something else to do. She put on her coat, gave her pale, tired face a rueful look in her compact mirror, renewed her lipstick and hurried down the stairs.

The door at the bottom opened as she reached out for the door handle.

Startled, Stephanie found herself staring at Gerard in a wig and gown, his austerely modelled features chilling in that formal frame. She froze, suddenly whisked back five years, to the courtroom where she had last seen him looking like that; his eyes accusing, harsh, his mouth taut and contemptuous.

'You're still here,' he said. 'Good, I wanted to talk to you. Come back upstairs—I have to change.'

'I'm sorry, I must go, I . . .'

'Don't argue, Stephanie.' He took her arm between

biting fingers and marched her back up the stairs. 'How did you get on today? Finding your feet?'

'I suppose so.'

He shot her a sideways look and his face relented a little. 'Don't sulk.'

'I'm tired, I've been here since nine this morning and everyone else has gone.'

'I'm not asking you to do any more work.' He drew her after him through the reception lobby along a narrow corridor lined with doors that led to the various offices of the barristers. Gerard pushed open the final door; she followed him into a square, dimly lit room containing little furniture but a desk, several chairs and a wall lined with books.

Gerard discarded his gown and wig, then sat down behind the desk in a black leather swivel chair, waving her to a chair on the other side of it. He considered her through the gloom. It was almost dark outside; she wondered why he didn't put on the light.

'Do you think you're going to enjoy working here?' He leaned back with his hands linked behind his fair head, and she tried not to watch him.

'I hope so.' Stephanie was guarded, unwilling to admit too much.

He put one polished black shoe on the desk and swivelled lazily in his chair, his long body totally relaxed. 'You had lunch with young Barry?' He made Barry sound insignificant, his tone derisory. 'I shouldn't encourage him; he's what Imogen calls a liberty-taker. He needs to be kept firmly under control.'

'I liked him,' Stephanie said defiantly, and saw a steely flash in his eyes.

'If he starts putting his arm around your waist on your first day, he'll be taking your clothes off by

Friday—or wouldn't you object to that?' The flinty grate of his voice contradicted the lazy posture of his body, and she sat up, startled, then became angry in her turn.

'I can manage Barry. He's rather nice.' She looked pointedly at her watch. 'I really must be going, I promised Julia I'd be back by six-thirty.'

Gerard was frowning, but he leaned forward, taking his foot off the desk. 'Did you come by car?'

'No, tube.'

'Very wise, parking is a nightmare around here. I managed to get a free meter half an hour ago, I'll give you a lift home.'

'I thought you'd been in court all afternoon.'

'I was. I should have said that I got an attendant from the private car park where I leave my car to bring it round here as soon as the rush hour slackened off. You can usually find a meter in this street by then; most people have left for home.'

Stephanie got up and Gerard rose too. 'It's very kind of you to offer, but there's no need to go out of your way for me.'

'No problem. Have dinner with me tonight.'

She had put a hand to the polished brass knob on his door. His hand immediately covered hers and she stiffened, warily becoming conscious that he was now behind her, his body touching hers.

'I can't, I'm sorry,' she stammered. 'Julia said something about cooking spaghetti tonight.'

'Julia won't mind if you ring and say you've got a date. She can cook spaghetti another night.' He moved closer, his shoulder warm against her. 'Have dinner with me, Stephanie, I haven't seen you for almost a week.' His voice was deep, low, intimate. It sent a disturbed quiver through her whole body.

'It's getting dark in here,' she muttered.

'Are you scared of the dark?'

She felt the hair rise on the back of her neck, and couldn't answer.

'Or of me?' he murmured, his mouth almost touching the nape of her neck, his breathing warm on her skin. 'It's easier to let your senses do their work in the dark, Stephanie; they aren't distracted by visual signals, they pick up other give-aways like the fact that you're trembling, for instance.

'I'm not,' she said huskily, trying to snap out of the sensual trance which was making her immobile. All she had to do was open the door and walk away from him. Why wasn't she doing that? Why was she standing here like a zombie and, come to that, why was he kissing her neck and sliding his arm around her waist? Why was she letting him get away with it? He had called Barry a liberty-taker; beside him, Barry's behaviour paled into insignificance.

'I've got to go,' she said vaguely, shivering at the feel of his mouth on her neck.

'I've missed you,' he said right into her ear; his teeth gently nibbled her lobe, but it wasn't his teeth that were giving her cause to worry, it was where his hand had got to—angrily she felt her breasts rounding, growing taut, their nipples hard against the thin material of her blouse. 'I thought we might have dinner somewhere special,' he suggested, hardly making a ripple on the surface of her mind. All she could think about was the deep, sensual passion that had gripped her body; waves of desire kept sweeping up into her head, making her forcibly aware of what was going on in the rest of her. He must know. He must hear her rapid, erratic breathing, feel the heat radiating from her.

The telephone began to ring. Gerard swore, giving a start she felt, his body tensing.

'Who the hell is that?' He opened his door. 'Let's go now, I'm not here, I don't want to talk to anybody.'

Stephanie was too dazed to argue or think straight. He swept her out of the building, down the street and into his big black Daimler. She was still blinking in the glare of the yellow street lamps after the darkness of his office, and didn't notice at first that he had turned northwards instead of heading for the river and Chelsea.

When she did realise it, she sat up in the seat, frowning. 'Where are you taking me? I'm not coming to Highgate—please, let me out up here. I'll get the tube from the next station.'

He drove on, ignoring her, and her nerves jumped and leapt with tension.

'I'm serious, Gerard. I'm not going to your house.'

'I want to talk to you,' was all he drawled.

'We have nothing to say to each other.'

'Oh, but we have.'

'What, for instance?' If only he would slow down, halt at some traffic lights, she could jump out and escape.

'Tell me about Theo Burgess.'

Stephanie turned cold. After a silence she said flatly, 'There's nothing to tell. Why must you keep going back to that?'

'I hate unsolved mysteries,' he said with a bitter dryness. 'That's probably why I'm a lawyer. I like to sort out the facts, understand them. So—tell me about Theo Burgess. Was he in love with you?'

'No. I told you—no! There was nothing going on between us, he was my employer, nothing more.'

'Viola must have got the idea from somewhere. She

wouldn't have killed him if she hadn't believed it.'

'She was unbalanced, and anyway, it wasn't . . .' She broke off and Gerard looked sharply at her.

'Anyway, what?'

She looked uncertainly at him. Would he believe her? Or would he think she had made the story up to convince him of her innocence? She decided to risk it; she couldn't be worse off than she was now.

'It wasn't Theo she was jealous about.'

Gerard had jerked to a halt at a set of traffic lights which had turned amber. She could have jumped out then and got away, but she had forgotten her plan. She was too intent on convincing him of the truth.

He turned to watch her intently. 'Who was it, then?'

'You.'

His eyes hardened, became fixed, the pupils glazed and glittering with anger.

'What the hell are you talking about?'

'It's the truth,' she said wearily. He wasn't going to believe her; she might have known it. 'That day when she killed Theo, she'd found me alone and started screaming at me to stay away from you, she said she'd fire me if I didn't stop dating you. She began hitting me, I fell over, and that was when Mr Burgess came in and ran over to help me.' Her voice had a flat monotonous sound; she told him what Theo had said, Viola's reaction, the shots. 'I thought she was going to kill me, too, she turned the gun towards me and I passed out. That was the last thing I remembered, but she was lying when she said we quarrelled over Theo—we didn't, it was you.'

Gerard was driving away from the traffic lights when her voice trailed into silence. She looked uncertainly at his rigid profile; the jaw unyielding, the mouth cold and straight. She didn't need to hear his voice to know he was angry; rage vibrated around him.

'You don't believe me, do you?' she whispered. 'I don't know why I told you the truth. Oh, let me out. I want to get away from you. I've had enough!'

He swerved over and stopped dead, almost sending her through the windscreen. Stephanie opened the door and stumbled out, and was hardly on the pavement when the car screeched away.

CHAPTER NINE

A week later, Joan left and Stephanie began running the outer office on her own. She adapted easily to the new routine; the work wasn't difficult, merely exacting, and she was interested in the people she met and the cases the firm handled. It was a more demanding job than the one she had had in the hotel, yet it was so much more varied and challenging that the longer hours and constant activity during the day only registered in the sense that she was far more tired when she left in the evening than she had ever been in her previous job.

She liked the people she was working with; even Imogen was a little more unbending now that Joan wasn't there to irritate her. As Stephanie began to streamline the filing and tidy the muddle Joan had left behind her, the outer office began to look much neater. Mr Beaumont congratulated her during her second week there. He had the grand air of an actor-manager, his smile gracious. 'Keep up the good work, Stephanie, we rely on you girls to keep us working at full pitch.'

When he had left, Barry imitated him. 'Keep up the good work, Stephanie!' He swept back a lock of hair with one of Mr Beaumont's theatrical gestures, preening. Stephanie laughed and Barry grinned. 'Feel like a show tonight, darling? We could have supper afterwards.' He perched on the edge of her desk and she looked ruefully at him, hunting for a kind way of refusing. Barry was rather an idiot and he was much

157

too young for her, but she liked him and didn't want to hurt his feelings.

'Get on with your work, Tomkins!' Gerard's voice hit them like a wind from the frozen north, and Barry jumped down and left in a hurry while Stephanie began to type, her gaze fixed on the shorthand notes in her pad. Gerard came over to stand behind her, watching, making her even more nervous.

'Haven't you finished those notes yet?'

'Almost.'

'I thought I warned you against encouraging that boy?'

'I wasn't.' She typed furiously, ignoring the mistakes she was making. She would have to go back and retype them when he was gone.

He suddenly caught hold of her wrists, lifting her hands from the keys and holding them up in the air, flapping limply. 'Look at me when I'm talking to you!'

'You told me to hurry with these notes, sir,' Stephanie reminded him angrily, and looked up. That was a mistake; he was bending and she hadn't realised how near he was. It gave her a shock, her pulses skipped a beat, her colour changed passionately, and Gerard took a deep, audible breath.

'Have dinner with me tonight,' he said huskily, holding her nervous eyes.

She shook her head mutely. She couldn't trust her voice.

'I have to see you,' he muttered, voice rough, his reluctance to admit as much all too clear.

'What's the point? You never believe a word I say. I've told you the truth, but you won't accept it.'

'I want to,' he said, his hands slackening their grip. He turned her hands over and stared down at the pink palms, one thumb gently touching each in an almost absentminded caress. 'If what you told me was true, why didn't you tell the court five years ago? Why didn't you challenge Viola's evidence?'

She looked up, then, sighing. 'I didn't want to drag you into it. I knew I was innocent as far as Theo was concerned and I knew Viola had shot him and might have shot me—I didn't think her threats about you had anything to do with it, and I didn't want to talk about it in front of a room full of strangers.'

'Even if it meant that your reputation was ruined?'

'I didn't realise it would be,' she whispered. 'It wasn't until I was in that court and saw your face, the way other people looked at me, that it dawned on me that I might not be on trial, but I'd been found guilty of something I hadn't done.'

He watched her intently, his brows heavy, but before he could say another word they heard someone coming up the stairs. Gerard let go of her and straightened.

'I'll pick you up at Julia's flat at eight,' he said, walking away.

When she got back to the flat that evening Julia was in the bath, singing. She broke off, mid-aria, to call, 'Hi, is that you?'

'What if I'd been a burglar?' asked Stephanie from outside the door, laughing.

'I'd have sat in this bath until it turned to ice,' Julia assured her. 'In to supper tonight? I'm going out with a fellow from the glassware firm I'm doing market research for—purely business, of course.'

'Of course,' Stephanie agreed, amused. Julia might miss her absent boy-friend, but she still managed to go out several times a week, always insisting that the dates were 'purely business'.

'Don't sound so dubious!' said Julia, laughing.

'Who, me?' Stephanie went into her own room and looked through her wardrobe for something to wear. She still hadn't made up her mind whether or not to go out to dinner with Gerard. It would probably mean another bitter argument, if she did. He had made up his mind about her and so far nothing she had said had been able to dissuade him. She didn't know why she bothered to try—he had pushed his way back into her life, but that didn't mean she had to care what he thought of her. Going out with him would only encourage him to believe he might seduce her, but he could think again. She had no intention of letting him talk her into his bed.

She heard Julia vacate the bathroom and went out, a towelling robe over her arm, to take a quick shower herself, before dressing. Julia paused as she was about to go into her bedroom and looked curious.

'You going out too?' Stephanie hadn't been out in the evening since she moved into the flat.

'Probably,' Stephanie said evasively, shutting the bathroom door before Julia could ask any more questions. They got on very well. Stephanie hadn't shared a flat with anyone before, but she found it easy to co-exist with Julia, who was good-tempered, easy-going and lively. All the same, she didn't want to talk to her about Gerard.

She ran the shower, stripped and stepped under the water, her eyes shut. Julia had told her a great deal about Gerard over the past few days, casual remarks at intervals about his family, his home, his background. It was obvious that Julia was fond of him; they teased each other and made fun of each other, but it was a sound relationship based on what seemed to be a healthy respect. Stephanie didn't want to say anything that might lead to a squabble between herself and Julia. If she so much as hinted that Gerard wasn't her idea of the perfect man, Julia might be offended. She seemed to have a romantic illusion about Gerard's interest in Stephanie.

As she stepped out of the shower, wrapping herself in her towelling robe, she heard the phone ringing. She opened the bathroom door and Julia called agitatedly. 'Answer that, will you? If it's for me, take a message. I'm trying to wriggle into a dress that seems to have shrunk. I'd swear I haven't gained an inch, but this damn thing won't slide over my hips.'

Stephanie smiled and walked into the small sitting-room. 'Hallo?' she asked, and had a slight shock as she heard her brother's voice.

'Stephanie?'

'Oh, hallo, Robert. How are you?' she said guardedly, wondering why he was ringing.

'I'm okay. How are you? Thanks for your letter. I'm glad the job's working out.'

'I'm enjoying it, it's very interesting. How's Gwen?'

'Fine.' Robert paused. 'Stephanie, Euan's back.'

'Oh.' Her hand tightened on the receiver.

'He's very angry. He wants to know where you are, he won't take no for an answer, Stevie.'

She bit her lip. 'You didn't tell him this address?'

'Not yet. I said I'd ask your permission first.'

Stephanie thought for a minute, frowning. 'Robert, couldn't you explain that I'd just decided it wouldn't work out between us? I really can't face him. There's no point.'

'Don't you think you owe it to him to talk to him face to face?'

'What can I say to him? You admitted yourself that his family would be horrified if they knew about the trial.'

'I suppose you're right,' Robert said uncertainly. 'But I'm sorry for Euan. Coming back from Saudi to find your letter waiting for him was a slap in the face.'

'I'm sorry, I wish there had been another way of dealing with it, I wish I hadn't had to do it like that, but I couldn't see anything else to do.' Stephanie was upset. Did Robert think she had acted without thinking? That she enjoyed hurting people? Didn't he realise that she had been hurt, too?

'I thought you were keen on Euan,' said Robert flatly.

She paled. 'I liked him very much.' She had almost been in love with Euan; in fact, she'd been pretty sure she was in love, but now she knew she hadn't been. She had never quite given herself to that relationship. Her early experience of love with Gerard had made her too wary to risk her deepest feelings without being totally certain the man was the right one. She hadn't wanted to get hurt again.

'He seems to have believed it was more serious than that,' said Robert with accusation in his voice.

Stephanie closed her eyes. 'I'm sorry.'

'Is that what I'm to tell him? That you're sorry but you just don't want to know any more?'

'Don't be angry, Rob,' she pleaded.

'Euan's a good friend of mine. What do you expect?' Robert breathed audibly for a second or two. 'Well, I'll try to make it easier on him, but it's just as well you've left here. Euan is angry enough to get violent.'

He hung up abruptly and Stephanie slowly replaced her phone, on the point of tears. She couldn't blame Robert for being angry; he must be having a difficult time with Euan. She couldn't blame Euan, either—he must have been thunderstruck when he got back and found her letter. They were both angry with her, and there was absolutely nothing she could say in her own defence except that she had been trying to protect them both from the consequences of her past.

The doorbell rang and she jumped. Julia gave a shriek from her room. 'Oh, no! Stevie—get that, will you? I'm in a tearing hurry to get out of here and I still haven't finished my make-up.'

Stephanie reluctantly opened the door, on the chain, so that the caller shouldn't see her in her short robe.

Gerard eyed her through the slit, his mouth ironic. 'Aren't you ready?'

She clutched the neck of her robe, shaking her head, keeping to one side of the partially opened door so that he could only see her face.

He studied it shrewdly, his face alert. 'What's the matter? Has something happened?'

'Nothing,' she said bitterly, her eyes diamond-bright with unshed tears. 'I feel as if I've been put through a wringer, that's all. My brother rang me. Euan's back and asking questions.' She broke off, starting to close the door. 'Oh, never mind—I'm really in no mood to go out to dinner, I'm sorry, Gerard.'

He had his foot in the door. 'Open up, Stephanie,' he said coolly. 'I'm not going away, so you might as well, or I'll keep ringing the bell and hammering on the door until you let me in.'

She looked at him in angry resignation. He meant it, he wouldn't hesitate to make a scene, force her to open the door.

'You're totally unscrupulous, aren't you?' she told him with dislike.

'Totally,' he agreed as she unhooked the chain. He was through the door a second later and she backed, only too aware of the fact that he had her at a disadvantage.

'I'm going to get dressed,' she said, not quite able to meet his eyes. They saw a damned sight too much; moving with the speed of lightning, from her damp hair, quivering mouth and pale throat down over her body to her bare legs and feet.

'Where's Julia?'

'Getting dressed herself, she's going out to dinner.' Stephanie could have kicked herself for telling him as she saw the gleam in his eye. She shouldn't have let him know she was going to be here alone all evening. She turned and hurried back to the shelter of her bedroom. At least she would be fully dressed next time she saw him.

She was brushing her hair when she heard Julia talking to him. 'Oh, you're here to collect Stevie, are you? I wondered who she had a date with.'

'Who else does she have dates with?' asked Gerard, and Julia laughed.

'Green eyes don't suit you, coz. And I don't tell tales. I like Stevie.'

Stephanie moved away from the door, her face a little more relaxed. She hadn't needed to hear Julia say she liked her, but she was glad she had. She liked Julia, too. She looked at herself in the mirror, wondering if the simple little white dress had been the right choice. It made her look demure, the neckline high and frilled in a sort of ruff, the sleeves long, billowing from the elbow to the cuff, the waist high, almost under her breasts, and the skirt straight and smoothly flowing over her hips. The only problem was that it also made her look younger, and she needed to impress Gerard with her self-assurance if she was to make him go away.

When she went back to the sitting-room she found

him alone. Stephanie looked around, frowning.
'Where's Julia?'

'She left to meet her date.' He was casually seated on
the couch, a glass of whisky in his hand. He had taken
off his dark overcoat and she could see that he was
wearing an elegant dark striped suit with a crisp white
shirt and maroon silk tie. His blond hair shone in the
lamplight, his eyes were thoughtful, speculative as
they roamed over her.

'You look charming,' he complimented. 'Sweet as
honey. Clothes can conceal a lot, can't they?'

'So can faces,' Stephanie said with bitterness.
'When I met Viola she seemed friendly and pleasant. I
never guessed that she was a manic depressive. People
are a lot more deceptive than clothes.'

He turned the glass in his hand, studying the amber
liquid as if he had never seen whisky before. 'That's
what I thought when I heard the rumours about you
and Theo Burgess. I was stunned. Do you think I
wanted to believe it? But think of the evidence—Viola
had shot her husband, killed him. The maid who ran
into the room when she heard the shots found Theo
lying on top of you. She thought Viola had shot both of
you at first. Viola swore she'd walked into the room to
find you in Theo's arms, she swore Theo had said he
was going to have her put away in a mental home so
that he could marry you. I heard all this from Viola,
but I heard it from the police and the servants too, and
it seemed to fit.'

'But you knew Viola wasn't normal! You knew she
had a history of mental illness.'

'That didn't make her a murderer. Her illness was
intermittent and even when she was in the manic
phase she'd never actually attacked anyone before.
She smashed furniture, windows—yes. But things

aren't people.' Gerard lifted the glass to his mouth and swallowed all the remaining whisky, then looked at her, his eyes darkened and glowing.

'And I was jealous. I was out of my mind with jealousy and disgust—the very thought of you with Theo Burgess made me sick. My judgement was warped by my own emotions.'

She sat down slowly, hardly daring to breathe. 'Are you saying that you believe me now?'

He put down the empty glass with a little click which made her nerves jump.

'Yes. I was never a hundred per cent sure even at the time, but I didn't get the chance to see you, talk about it.'

'You didn't try!'

'I did, in the beginning. I went to see your parents and they said you couldn't see anyone. The police knew I was working with the defence team. They didn't want your evidence to be influenced by anyone connected with Viola Burgess. I couldn't see you until the trial, and then in the witness box you admitted that Theo had called you his little love, and it seemed conclusive, it was such a damaging admission. There could only be one explanation—Theo must have been in love with you.'

'I'm sure he wasn't,' Stephanie broke out, flushing hotly. 'He never gave me a hint, not a look, not a word . . .'

'Perhaps he knew he didn't have a chance with you but that doesn't mean he wasn't in love with you. He was an unhappy, lonely man. You were young and pretty and he saw you every day. It would have been natural enough for him to be attracted to you.'

She lowered her eyes and couldn't think of anything

to say. It made her miserable to think of Theo. The tragedy had brushed her life and darkened it for years; it still affected her.

'What was all that about your brother ringing you?' Gerard asked flatly.

'He wanted to tell me that Euan was back and demanding to know where I was.' She sighed, a wrenched sigh that made her slender body shudder. 'It's so unfair! I didn't do anything wrong. I was just in the wrong place at the wrong time, quite innocently, but because of that one tragic coincidence I can't seem to escape from the past. I don't know what to do. I asked Robert to tell Euan I was sorry but I couldn't see him again. So Robert's angry with me. He can't deny that there's no other way of dealing with the situation, and his job might suffer if anyone found out about the trial, but he still blames me, I know he does. Robert's angry with me, Euan's angry with me—it simply isn't fair!'

Gerard watched her intently. 'Are you in love with Cameron?'

She didn't answer.

'Stephanie, are you? Tell me!'

'What difference does it make if I am?'

'I could see Cameron for you, explain, give him the chance to choose.' His voice was cool and clear, almost remote. It shocked her into looking up again incredulously.

'I thought you were the one who said I ought to go away? You blackmailed me into leaving him.'

'I shouldn't have done that,' he said as though it was a purely academic question they were discussing. 'Whenever you come into a situation I stop thinking rationally and make emotional decisions. When I saw that letter from Mrs Cameron and realised that I'd found you again, that you were apparently on the point of marrying her son, I guessed at once that you hadn't told him about the Burgess case. I've known the Camerons for years—I know the sort of people they are, and I couldn't imagine Margo Cameron being happy about her son marrying a girl with a sordid scandal in her background. So I told myself that it was my duty to go down there and put a stop to any idea of marriage between you and Cameron.' His mouth twisted in self-distaste. 'Oh, I convinced myself that I had the most impeccable reasons for smashing up your love affair. I was full of self-righteous indignation about you lying to the Camerons, hiding your past from them, but of course the truth was that I was jealous. I couldn't bear the idea of Cameron having you.'

A pulse beat fiercely in her neck. 'But now you're offering to bring us together again!'

'I want you to be sure what you want,' said Gerard brusquely. 'When I first read that letter to my mother and realised who it was about I had a rush of blood to the head. After the trial I was too angry to want to see you, but I didn't forget you. I kept thinking back over everything and being puzzled and uncertain about the whole story. One day I'd be sure Viola was telling the truth, another time I'd remember your innocence and I couldn't believe you would ever have had an affair with Theo. That's what I meant about being bedevilled by emotion. I wasn't thinking with my head, I was too bitter and jealous. I thought with my heart, and that never works. Love is a violent emotion; it can destroy, it can smash lives the way a hurricane smashes a whole town. I shouldn't have let my feelings dominate my thinking.'

'Whatever your reasons for interfering,' she said

slowly, 'you were right about Euan and his family. I couldn't see him again without telling him the whole story, and once he knows I don't think he would still want me.'

'But with your family and myself to back your version?'

'If I brought an archangel and several judges to back me up, I don't think Mrs Cameron would want me in her family, do you? I'd still have a slur on my name.'

'Stephanie, if you love him . . .'

'I don't,' she said flatly. 'I told you that last time you asked. My heart isn't broken because I won't see Euan again. I'll miss him. I liked him, I was fond of him, I might even have loved him enough to marry him one day, but it wasn't the violent kind of love, not the kind you were talking about. I didn't think with my heart where Euan was concerned. I felt with my head, and I wonder if that isn't just as bad?'

His mouth had a crooked humour and his eyes smiled. 'You may be right.' He moved suddenly, along the couch, his arm going around her. 'Stephanie . . .'

She got up. 'I thought we were going to dinner?'

Gerard stiffened, watching her, then shrugged and got up too. 'Of course. I booked a table at the Caprice.'

'I'll just get my jacket,' she said, and went back into her bedroom. The last thing she needed at the moment was for Gerard to try to kiss her. She needed time to think, or rather, to separate thought and emotion, understand how she really felt.

She had been hiding things from herself right from the first moment when she saw Gerard again outside the hotel. The shock of that first sight of him should have told her how much he still affected her, but she hadn't wanted to believe it.

Until that day she had been thinking herself into a state of blissful deception, convincing herself that she could love Euan, marry him. She had built a new life for herself; it was calm and tranquil and safe, but she had blinded herself to the fact that it was built on sand. She hadn't simply omitted to tell Euan and his family about an unpleasant episode in her past; she had lied to herself when she pretended she had forgotten Gerard and no longer cared about him. You can't build a life on lies.

Seeing Gerard again had brought her phoney paradise into sharp, realistic focus, shown her the truth about herself. Her reaction to Gerard had been so intense and passionate, a chemical change that was physically violent. She had gone hot, then cold, she had been white and then flushed—her emotions had gone crazy. She had been off balance ever since. Compared to her calm and civilised relationship with Euan, that white-hot emotional drag towards Gerard had been little short of catastrophic. It had blown to smithereens her cosy self-deception.

But she didn't want Gerard to know all this—he might suspect how she felt, but while he wasn't certain he wouldn't really turn the heat on.

She wasn't going to run away from her feelings, but she had been invaded by a sense of panic in case Gerard rushed her. How could she think when her chemical reaction to his presence had such a disturbing effect on her mental processes? She wondered if Gerard even understood himself—she didn't understand him. She didn't know what he really wanted from her—a satisfaction he hadn't got five years ago? A delayed revenge for the frustration he had felt then? She didn't need to wonder if he wanted her; her feminine instincts had warned her about that from the minute he had walked back into her life. She was five years older and five years wiser, especially about men. Gerard wanted her, but why?

Until she knew the answer to that, until she knew whether *she* felt more than a violent physical desire for him, she would have to try to keep him at a distance.

That wouldn't be easy, she accepted with a qualm of nerves, as she rejoined him and Gerard's grey eyes fixed a brilliant, triumphant gleam on her. She picked up the excitement in him without any trouble, and her body clenched. How was she going to deal with him in this mood?

CHAPTER TEN

THAT dinner seemed to drag on endlessly. She had never been so on edge in her life, her senses piercingly aware of every move he made, every intonation in his voice, every passing expression in his eyes. They were seated on either side of a table, a few feet apart, but her heart did a nosedive every time their eyes met.

Gerard suddenly stretched out a hand holding the menu and blocked her view of her plate. 'What are you eating?'

Stephanie glanced down and could only see the menu. 'What are you talking about?' she hedged. 'Don't be silly!'

'Tell me what's on your plate,' he insisted, eyes mocking.

'I'm not playing one of your games.' She tried to remember what she had just swallowed. Fish. She was sure it had been fish, although her attention hadn't been on what she was putting into her mouth. It had all been riveted on Gerard; she might just as well have been eating sawdust.

'Fish,' she said coolly. 'I'm eating fish.'

He took the menu away and she hurriedly looked down. There was a médaillon of veal on her plate in a delicate creamy sauce. Gerard laughed softly and her cheeks burned.

'Well, I was thinking about something else,' she said crossly.

'I know, so was I,' he murmured, a glint in his eye. 'It was when I realised that I didn't have a clue what I was eating that I looked across and saw the same blank look on your face.'

'I wasn't really hungry,' she said with dignity. 'I didn't want to have dinner out, but it seemed . . .' Her voice faltered.

'Safer than staying in?' he finished for her with a dry smile. 'I deduced as much. It's true that there are fewer opportunities for making love in a restaurant than there are in an empty flat.'

The waiter came to take their plates and overheard that. He gave Gerard an interested look and an even more interested glance at Stephanie, who looked down, biting her inner lip.

'A dessert, madam?' asked the waiter.

'No, thank you,' she refused with vehemence.

'Coffee for both of us,' Gerard ordered, and they didn't sit for long drinking it. Half an hour later they were in Gerard's car driving back to her flat, and neither of them had much to say. Stephanie knew what he was thinking; the car was full of a tense silence vibrating with feeling and when he pulled up outside the flat she said hurriedly 'No need to get out. Thank you for dinner. I'll see you tomorrow.'

He caught her arm as she turned to get out. 'Stephanie . . .'

She threw him an uneasy look over her shoulder, her dark hair blown across her eyes by the night wind. 'Please, don't,' she said huskily. 'I'm too tired, I can't take any more.'

She thought for a moment that he was going to ignore what she said, ride roughshod over her plea to be left alone, but although his brows drew together his hand dropped, allowing her to get out of the car. She began to walk quickly towards the building, hearing the car engine flare into life again.

Just as she reached the front door a figure stepped out of the shadows and grabbed her, and Stephanie gave a cry of shock.

For a second she thought it was a stranger, a mugger, grabbing for her handbag, but then he moved and the light of the street lamp shone full on his face.

It was Euan. 'I've been waiting for over an hour,' he said roughly. 'Where have you been?'

She glanced over her shoulder and saw Gerard's car moving off. Her body sagged in a sort of relief. At least he wouldn't be present at what was bound to be a difficult interview, thank heavens she hadn't invited him in for coffee, or rather, allowed him to invite himself, which was probably what had been on his mind when he caught her arm just now.

She looked back at Euan with uneasy regret. 'You'd better come in—we can't talk on the doorstep.' She led the way and unlocked the front door of the flat. It was dark. Obviously Julia was still out at dinner, but she was bound to get back before too long and Stephanie didn't want her to find Euan in the flat.

She switched on the light and Euan followed her into the flat, closing the door behind himself.

'You haven't driven all that way this evening?' she asked as she switched on the light in the sitting-room.

'Yes, I left at seven-thirty and got here at almost nine-thirty, but there was no answer so I've been sitting in my car waiting for you ever since. I saw you drive up with your friend.' His voice flattened on the final word and she felt him watching her intently, although she didn't look in his direction.

'Please sit down,' she said huskily. 'Can I get you anything? A drink? Coffee?'

'I wouldn't say no to a whisky.' He took off his overcoat and laid it over a chair, then sat down, crossing his legs.

Stephanie hunted for the bottle of whisky Julia kept in a cupboard and poured a little into a glass. There was no soda, so she asked if Euan would like some water in it, but he shook his head.

She gave him the whisky and sat down nervously, not too close to him.

'How did you find me?' she queried.

'Your brother told me your address.'

Her eyes widened in anger and shock. Robert had promised he wouldn't tell Euan!

He swallowed a mouthful of whisky, watching her. 'Yes, I know you asked him not to tell me where you were—but I managed to persuade him otherwise.' His eyes had an impatient darkness in them. 'I practically had to choke it out of him. I told him if he didn't explain what was going on, I'd get a private detective to dig you out, I wasn't just accepting this meekly. So then he told me the whole story.'

Her eyes flew to his face in shock. 'The whole . . .'

Euan stared back at her gently, his face softening. 'The whole story, all about the trial, the murder, the accusations against you—my God, Stephanie, you must have a low opinion of me if you really thought I'd believe that you would have an affair with a man twice your age! I know you better than that and I'd hoped you knew me better.' He drank a little more whisky, then sat staring into the glass, his face sombre. 'I can understand why you wouldn't want it to become public knowledge, why you'd hate the thought of strangers talking about you, but why didn't you trust me, Stephanie? Didn't you feel you knew me well enough to confide in me instead of bolting like this?'

She looked down, shifting unhappily in the chair. 'I'm sorry if you're hurt, Euan. That was the last thing

I intended, but I couldn't stay. Not once I'd realised that it wouldn't do. You may not believe that I had an affair with Theo Burgess, but a lot of other people did believe it, and if any of them turned up in town and started spreading the story it would be very embarrassing for your family. Your mother wouldn't want to be mixed up with someone like me.'

'Leave my mother out of it,' Euan said tersely. 'It's my opinion that matters, not hers.'

'Is it?' she asked on a sigh. Didn't Euan realise how much his family mattered to him?

'I want you to come back with me,' Euan said firmly. 'You can't run from something like this. You have to face it, you have to be brave, Stephanie.'

She smiled wryly. 'I'm sorry, Euan, it wouldn't work. There's no point.'

'You don't need to worry about my mother. She'll come round once she realises I'm serious about you. If there's trouble, we'll face it together.'

He was so civilised, so reasonable, but in a way he was blind to the truth about his family situation. He was reacting now with awareness of what was the proper thing to do; Stephanie had run away because she feared public opinion in a very conservative little community, and Euan's sense of justice wouldn't allow her to suffer because of something she hadn't done. He was prepared to fight for her, face his mother for her, but he was ignoring the truth—that his family, his mother, mattered more to him than she did. If she had doubted that for a second she wouldn't have run away. It was because Gerard had made her face that, that she had left.

He put down his glass and came over to her chair, sat down on the arm of it, and stroked her wind-ruffled hair gently. 'I want you to marry me, Stephanie. I've been meaning to ask you for a long time, but I'm asking you now. You must know how much you mean to me. I think we could be very happy together and . . .'

The doorbell rang violently and she jumped. Euan stopped in mid-flow, his hand stiffening on her hair.

'Who can that be at this hour?' He looked down at her as the bell continued to peal. Whoever was out there had left his thumb on the button. 'Is that the girl who shares your flat? She must have forgotten her key.'

Stephanie knew it wasn't Julia; she knew whose thumb was jammed down on the button. She didn't want to open the door to him, not while Euan was here. It would only mean trouble, and she was so sick of argument and fight and threats.

'Ignore it,' she said, very agitated.

Euan looked amazed. 'Ignore it? You can't do that.'

'It will go away.'

'Have you quarrelled with your flatmate already? But I thought this was her flat. You can't leave her on the doorstep, whatever she's done.'

'It isn't her, not Julia,' she said in confusion. 'Oh, take no notice, he'll give up in a minute.'

Euan stiffened. 'He?' He seized on the pronoun sharply, looking down at her. 'Stephanie, who's out there?'

Suddenly she knew that Robert had carefully omitted one vital part of the story. He hadn't told Euan about Gerard Tenniel's intervention, he hadn't mentioned that Gerard had brought her to London, that she had been in Gerard's house when Robert caught up with her the day she left town.

Why had Robert been so discreet? But she knew the answer to that, didn't she? Her brother hadn't wanted

Euan to be aware that she was mixed up with Gerard
Tenniel, but if Euan forced her to open the front door
now, he would soon realise what Robert had gone to
such pains to keep from him.

'Nobody,' she said, very flushed. The ringing hadn't
stopped; it was now augmented by some angry
hammering on the door. It sounded ominously as if
Gerard was trying to break into the flat.

'It sounds very much like a persistent somebody,'
said Euan, still staring at her. 'If you want me to get rid
of whoever it is, I'll be glad to deal with him for you.'
He got up and she shot to her feet, grabbing his hand.

'No Euan, don't go out there!'

'Why not?' he asked reasonably enough, his eyes
puzzled and beginning to be distinctly suspicious.
'Have you met someone else, Stephanie? Is that it?
Another man? Robert didn't warn me about that. Or
is this a neighbour who won't take no for an answer?
There must be a good reason why you don't want to
answer the door.'

She tried to think of one, her face distraught, but her
mind wasn't working fast enough. Euan walked away,
dragging her after him, her heels grinding into the
carpet at every step.

'Euan, please don't!' she wailed as he put a hand on
the latch, but she was too late. He had opened the door
and Gerard fell into the flat, taken by surprise. He
must have been trying to shoulder his way through the
door.

Euan looked staggered. Gerard didn't. Once he had
recovered his balance he said angrily 'If I hadn't
glanced into my driving mirror just before I got to the
corner, I wouldn't have seen him. I had to drive right
round the block before I could get back here, because
of this damned one-way system, and then I couldn't

find anywhere to park.'

'What are you doing here?' demanded Euan, having got his breath back.

'Snap,' Gerard said drily. 'I was just going to ask you the same question.'

'I didn't know you knew Stephanie!'

Gerard smiled; it was a deliberately provocative smile and it had the effect intended. Euan's face stiffened and reddened. He didn't have a belligerent nature, but he had a very male dislike of being laughed at and he vaguely realised that Gerard was making fun of him.

'Why were you ringing the bell like that at this hour?' he demanded, his hands screwing into fists.

'I wanted to come in,' said Gerard with silken mockery. He turned his eyes on Stephanie. 'Why didn't you open the door right away? What was going on?'

He had drawn Euan's attention back to her. Before she could answer him, Euan asked tersely: 'Why's he here? You only met him once, at our house, didn't you?' He paused, obviously thinking. 'Wait a min-ute—he said something about driving away and coming back—was that his car you drove up in? Had you been out with him tonight? Have you been seeing him since you came to London?' His usually calm expression had broken up in lines of anger and disbelief, he was looking at her in a way that distressed her.

'Do you suppose these are rhetorical questions?' Gerard asked her ironically. 'He doesn't stop long enough to give you a chance to answer, does he?'

Euan ignored him, his eyes on Stephanie's pale face. 'Did you come to London because of him? Am I to gather that Robert did *not* tell me the whole story?'

Gerard whistled softly. 'Oh, I see! Your brother decided to spill the beans!'

Euan swung round to glare at him. 'Does that mean you know all about this?' Apparently he read the answer in Gerard's cool eyes, because he turned back to Stephanie, looking even angrier. 'You told him, but you didn't tell me?' That seemed to stick in his throat, and she could understand why, her body wrenched by a deep sigh.

'Euan, I'm sorry, it isn't quite what you think.'

Gerard was smiling. 'A canny fellow, your brother—he was careful not to spill all the beans, obviously.' He was watching her face shrewdly, reading her reactions. 'If you've been having any hassle from him, let me deal with him,' he said quietly, touching her arm. 'You don't have to put up with any nonsense from him.'

Euan made a growling sound in his throat, poised on the balls of his feet as if about to hit Gerard.

'Oh, why did you come back?' Stephanie burst out to Gerard, her eyes angry. She felt like pushing both of them out of the flat, but she knew that that would merely postpone the inevitable. Euan was here and he had to have an answer, an explanation. It was Gerard who was the real problem, but she would deal with him when she felt up to it. She didn't feel up to it at the moment. 'Go away!' she almost snarled. 'I want to talk to Euan and I don't want you here!'

Gerard stared fixedly at her; the pupils of his eyes dilated until they were enormous, black, hard with anger.

Euan held the door open. 'You heard her.'

Gerard slowly turned and walked out and Euan let the door slam after him, before turning back to Stephanie with cold eyes.

'You don't need to tell me anything you don't want me to know. Obviously, I made a stupid mistake. Your brother should have been a little less discreet. I thought this business of the trial was the only problem; I didn't realise there was another man in your life now.'

She could have explained the whole complicated tangle, but she saw suddenly how much simpler it was to let him go away believing she had left because she had fallen in love with another man. It would make it easier for Euan. He wouldn't need to wonder if he ought to face a break with his family for her sake. She wasn't in love with him, but he might have felt he had to try to talk her into going back with him.

'I'm sorry, Euan,' she said.

'I had a wasted journey, didn't I?' He was looking at her; disillusion in his eyes, as though he had never really known her, and perhaps he hadn't. She had never really known herself. The years since the trial had been ostrich years, a period when she hid herself from sight and refused to see what was happening around her. She had been afraid to lift her head, but it was time she did.

'I'm afraid you did. I told Robert that it would be best just to let me slip away.' She looked quickly at him. 'Euan, for Robert's sake, don't tell anyone, even your mother—you haven't told your mother yet, have you?'

'No,' he agreed flatly.

'His reputation is more important than mine. I wouldn't want to jeopardise his career.'

'You won't. Everyone at the hospital thinks very highly of Robert. I had no intention of spreading this story, anyway, but you can have my word on it if you need it.' Euan was on his dignity now; he had withdrawn from her. She recognised the remoteness of his face; that was how his mother looked. Euan was very like his mother. Even if Gerard Tenniel had never come along to break them apart, she saw suddenly that she wouldn't have been happy with Euan, because sooner or later she would have had to tell him about the trial. You can't live with a lie for ever. And when she did tell him he would have looked at her the way he was looking at her now—as though she was a disappointment to him. He might have been kind and forgiving, but he wouldn't have trusted her after that.

He'd said that he believed she was innocent, but what was hidden in the very far reaches of his mind? A doubt? He had jumped so quickly to the belief that she was having an affair with Gerard now. Why should he be so ready to believe that if he didn't wonder how much truth there was in Viola Burgess's accusations?

He opened the front door to go and she saw Gerard leaning against the wall out there. He hadn't left; he was waiting. Euan's eyes flashed to him and his mouth indented distastefully.

Gerard came towards them at a stride. 'You aren't taking her with you,' he said harshly. 'She's mine!'

'So I gather,' said Euan from a great height, his face contemptuous as he glanced back at Stephanie.

Gerard didn't like the way he looked at her. He gave a furious snarl, shoulders hunched, and hit Euan, who ducked as he saw the punch coming. Gerard got him, all the same, a glancing blow on the jaw that sent Euan reeling backwards.

'No, Euan, don't hit him—your hands!' Stephanie cried out with horror.

Euan gritted through his teeth, 'I had no intention

of risking an injury to my hands.' He turned and walked away and Gerard stared after him in disgust.

'He's a surgeon; his hands are vital to his work,' Stephanie accused angrily. 'How could you, Gerard?'

'He insulted you.'

'He was angry, can you blame him?'

She turned and walked back into her flat and Gerard came too. 'Oh, why don't you go home and give me some peace?' she implored, turning on him as she realised he was in the flat again.

'Is he coming back?' he merely asked.

She gave him a bitter stare. 'Well, what do *you* think?'

He considered her fixedly. 'Did you want him to go? Or have you realised you do care for him?'

'I'm sick of talking about it. Go home, Gerard.'

'Not until I know where I stand!'

'Where *you* stand? You were asking about Euan.'

'Now that you've seen him again, how do you feel about him?' he asked curtly, still watching her with that intent gaze.

Stephanie looked away. 'How dare you tell him that I'm yours? You must have known what he'd make of that, then you say he's insulting me because he assumed what I think you meant him to assume—that I've been sleeping with you!'

'That wasn't what I meant, and he had no right to assume anything of the kind.' Gerard moved nearer, his voice dropping, becoming husky. 'You belong to me, you have ever since the first day I saw you. I don't need to sleep with you to say that you're mine.' He stood there, watching her. Very flushed, her eyes lowered, she could hardly breathe and wished he would stop staring. 'You can feel it, too, can't you?' he murmured, even closer now.

'No,' she whispered.

'Liar.' He wasn't touching her, but he was so close that she could hear his breathing, the rapid beat of his heart.

She closed her eyes to shut out the sight of that insistent face. 'Oh, why don't you stop tormenting me?'

'You're the one doing the tormenting,' Gerard whispered, kissing her eyelids gently one after the other. His lips brushed like butterflies, making her lashes flicker, sending a tingling feeling through her nervous system.

'Julia will be home any second,' she protested, taking hold of his arms to push him away. He didn't so much as move an inch; it was like trying to push over the rock of Gibraltar.

'Julia never gets home this early when she goes dancing. She told me she was getting back at the crack of dawn.' Gerard was lightly sliding his lips down her face, making for her mouth.

'You shouldn't be here!' she wailed. She had refused to let him come in earlier because she had known this would happen; she had seen it in his eyes, felt it inside herself. All evening they had been looking at each other with rapt attention; all evening she had been on edge, weak with desire, and Gerard had known. His eyes had warned her that he knew. She turned her head away before he could kiss her and he kissed her ear instead, biting gently at her lobe.

'I want you so badly, Stephanie,' he muttered, burying his face against her throat. 'I love you. I fell head over heels the first time I saw you and because of my own jealous stupidity I've wasted five years of my life. Don't waste any more of our precious time, darling.'

She made a helpless little moaning noise, swaying against him. He wasn't being fair, he was rushing her before she had had time to think it out, to be sure what she felt.

'I'm not sure yet,' she told him, aware of his arm round her, his hands touching her, his mouth advancing stealthily towards her lips.

'Sure about what? Marrying me? Whether you love me?' He took hold of her chin and turned her face back towards him. His mouth took hers before she could evade it and she yielded, her arms going round his neck, her body giving in to him under the insistent pressure of a hand in the small of her back. She stopped resisting, trying to think, she was all feeling; a rush of fierce pleasure swamping everything else.

Gerard suddenly lifted her off the ground and carried her into the sitting-room. He sat down on the couch and she found herself lying across his lap. He was still kissing her and she could hardly breathe; the remorseless demand of his mouth left her limp, suffocated. When he finally lifted his head, she just lay there, her head on his shoulder, her body tumbled along the couch.

She forced her lids up and he was bending over her, watching her with a probing intensity.

'I love you,' he said again, his voice rough, and Stephanie could see that she had nowhere left to hide.

'Love me—or want me?' she asked huskily. 'You told me you wanted me, that day in the hotel, when you blackmailed me into coming away with you. You made it clear you wanted your revenge; you didn't mention love then. How do I know you mean it now? How do I know this isn't another form of blackmail, meant to persuade me to sleep with you?'

His mouth went crooked. 'I was too angry and

jealous that day to be ready to admit I was still in love with you. I'd seen you with Cameron the night before, remember? I was afraid you'd marry him if I didn't get you away at once. I had to use sledgehammer methods, but I was certain you didn't love him. I was so sure you belonged to me. The minute I saw you, at the party, I felt it again—a drag between us, an instant flare of awareness. Don't tell me you didn't feel it, too, Stephanie, because I wouldn't believe you. You knew—I saw it in your eyes.'

She looked away, trembling. 'Is it love, though? That need.'

She heard his breathing quicken. He kissed her neck, mouth urgent, passionate. 'A need, darling, yes, that's just what it is—all lovers need to show what they feel, get that feeling back. When I first met you, you were just a girl and I thought I loved you simply because you were so inexperienced and innocent, but I was wrong. I love you far more passionately now; haven't you felt how much stronger it is, this feeling between us? Every beat of my heart makes it stronger.' He held her close to him, their bodies merging. 'Like this,' he muttered into her hair. 'We belong like this, darling, part of each other, for ever.'

He was right. She had known, from the minute she saw him again, that he was the only man she had ever loved and would ever love. Euan had become a shadowy figure to her after that, although she had tried to go on pretending for a while longer. It had been no use; no other man could ever mean as much to her. Gerard had been imprinted on her heart five years ago when she was too young and plastic for that deep seal ever to be removed.

She and Gerard belonged to each other. Even if she hadn't said it aloud her body was telling him so now, the heat of desire melting her flesh, burning through her senses. His hands were aware of that, she heard him breathing thickly, felt the heat in his face as his cheek brushed hers.

'Darling,' he said again, and he was asking her to admit it, to tell him. He was urgent because of the waste of five years, urgent as she was, because they needed to touch, to merge, to be one.

'I love you,' she said, and after that neither of them said anything for a long time.

Harlequin Presents

Coming Next Month

Available in July wherever paperback books are sold, or through Harlequin Reader Service:

In the U.S.
901 Fuhrmann Blvd.
P.O. Box 1397
Buffalo, N.Y. 14240-1397

In Canada
P.O. Box 603
Fort Erie, Ontario
L2A 5X3

Take 4 best-selling love stories FREE
Plus get a FREE surprise gift!

All men wanted her,
but only one man would have her.

Desert Storm
Nan Ryan

Her cruel father had intended
Angie to marry a sinister cattle baron twice her age.
No one expected that she would fall in love with his
handsome, pleasure-loving cowboy son.

Theirs was a love no desert storm would quench.

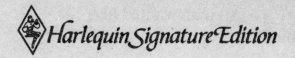

Carole Mortimer

Merlyn's Magic

She came to him from out of the storm and was drawn into his yearning arms—the tempestuous night held a magic all its own.

You've enjoyed Carole Mortimer's Harlequin Presents stories, and her previous bestseller, *Gypsy*.

Now, don't miss her latest, most exciting bestseller, *Merlyn's Magic*!

IN JULY

MERMG